Survival Squad: the series

Out of Bounds
Search and Rescue
Night Riders
White Water

SURVIVAL SQUAD

NIGHT RIDERS

JONATHAN ROCK

RED FOX

With thanks to Paul May

SURVIVAL SQUAD: NIGHT RIDERS
A RED FOX BOOK 978 1 862 30967 8

First published in Great Britain by Red Fox,
an imprint of Random House Children's Publishers UK
A Random House Group Company

This edition published 2013

1 3 5 7 9 10 8 6 4 2

The Random House Group Limited supports the Forest Stewardship Council
(FSC®), the leading international forest certification organization. Our books
carrying the FSC label are printed on FSC® certified paper. FSC is the only forest
certification scheme endorsed by the leading environmental organizations,
including Greenpeace. Our paper procurement policy can be found at
www.randomhouse.co.uk/environment.

Set in 13/19 pt Goudy by Falcon Oast Graphic Art Ltd.

Red Fox Books are published by Random House Children's Publishers UK,
61–63 Uxbridge Road, London W5 5SA

www.**randomhousechildrens**.co.uk
www.**totallyrandombooks**.co.uk
www.**randomhouse**.co.uk

Addresses for companies within The Random House Group Limited can be found
at: www.randomhouse.co.uk/offices.htm

THE RANDOM HOUSE GROUP Limited Reg. No. 954009

A CIP catalogue record for this book is available from the British Library.

Printed and bound in Great Britain by
CPI Group (UK) Ltd, Croydon, CR0 4YY

CHAPTER 1

Connor Sutcliff stood high on the ridge, looking down into the valley. The river was a silver snake far below, glinting in the sun. It was a long way down, and Connor fought to control his nerves.

'Are you ready, Connor?' asked the instructor, James, from behind him. James was a skinny guy with long blond hair and an infectious smile.

'Ready!' Connor replied, taking a deep breath. He could hear the wind inflating the long curved wing behind him and lifting it into the air. Ahead of him was a short stretch of rough grass, and then the ridge dropped steeply towards the valley. Away to one side, the other members of Tiger Patrol were watching eagerly as they awaited their own turns.

'Go!' yelled James. 'Run! That's it. Here we go!'

Suddenly they were in the air. Connor heard a ragged chorus of cheers from below and looked down to see the Tigers waving madly. Julie, their Assistant Scout Leader, was with them. She was a slim, athletic sports enthusiast and, more importantly, a seasoned paraglider. It had been Julie who had organized today's activities for the Sixth Matfield Scout Troop, and it looked as if it might just be their best day out ever.

In the sky ahead of him, against a background of fluffy white clouds and blue sky, Connor could see the shapes of five – no, six – other paragliders swooping through the air.

'I bet you've never been this high before,' James's voice said in his ear, over the rushing sound of the wind.

Connor looked down. The figures on the ridge were tiny now, and the road in the valley just a narrow black line with cars moving along it like multi-coloured beetles. 'Only in a plane,' he replied as James altered the position of his hands and the paraglider made a wide turn to the left.

'And that was nothing like this. Hey, look at those swifts! What are they doing?'

Above them, and slightly to their right, a flock of small fork-tailed birds were flying in tight circles, rising quickly through the air.

'Good spot!' said James. 'You've just found us a thermal, Connor. Or those swifts have. Let's go up!'

'What do you mean?' asked Connor.

Then James turned the wing again and the earth seemed to tilt beneath them.

'The sun warms the land down there,' James said. 'Then the hot air rises. Birds are great at finding thermals. Especially swifts. I love them – they really know how to fly! Let's see how high this one takes us. Here we go! Listen to that!'

Connor just had time to remember Julie explaining to them about thermals before the high-pitched beeps coming from a small device strapped to James's arm suddenly accelerated and he tilted the paraglider. 'Imagine you're riding a bike,' he yelled. 'We lean into the turn.'

As they turned round and round in the rising air of the thermal, the landscape fell away rapidly below them. Connor saw the distant smudge of a big city, and beyond the city the faint blue shadows of faraway mountains. And then, all at once, James left the thermal and sent them into a long downward glide.

'Sorry, Connor,' he said. 'That was a really good one you found us, but your mates are waiting for their turn.'

They zigzagged downwards and Connor picked out the ridge where the others were standing. Lower down he saw a line of Scouts making their way up the hillside from where they had been climbing on the crags. Until today, rock climbing had been Connor's favourite thing, but he knew he'd never be able to forget the experience of soaring through the sky like a bird.

Suddenly he realized that the ground was much closer. He could see the upturned faces of the other Tigers and the helpers. James had told him that they might have to run a few steps when they came down, but he circled round, came up into the wind and spilled air from the wing so skilfully that landing was no harder than stepping off a train. Connor's legs felt like jelly as he was helped out of his harness.

'You look ridiculously happy,' Abby said. 'Just wait till you see your face. That is the biggest smile I've ever seen!'

Abby was one of Connor's oldest friends. Her long brown hair was blowing in the wind and she held her helmet in one hand, ready for her turn. Connor knew that she would love paragliding as much as he did. Meanwhile her best friend, Andy, was aiming a camcorder at Connor's face.

Andy, often mistaken for Abby's twin, was a really talented photographer and was never without his favourite camera or camcorder. 'Can we have a few words for the camera?' he asked in his best TV interviewer's voice, flicking his brown hair out of his eyes. 'Can you describe the experience of paragliding for us?'

'It was just totally . . . incredibly . . .' Connor

paused. He couldn't think of a big enough word. 'You wait,' he said at last. 'You wait till you've tried it.'

'And I'm going to,' said Abby. 'Right now. I'm ready,' she said to James. 'What do I have to do?'

Connor joined the other Tigers. Jay and Priya, who had only joined the Scouts last September, were both looking a little apprehensive as they watched Abby being strapped into her harness. James completed his final checks, and seconds later Abby gave a scream of excitement as the inflated wing carried her into the sky.

'It's not as scary as it looks,' Connor told Priya and Jay reassuringly.

'I'm not scared,' Jay began; then he paused and grinned. 'Well, OK, I am a bit, but only like when you go on a big roller coaster.'

'That's how I feel too,' said Priya, her big brown eyes shining. 'And it wouldn't be exciting if it wasn't a bit scary, would it?'

Connor smiled. Priya was the youngest of the Tigers, but she loved a challenge. Even though she was wearing the same Scout uniform as the rest of them, she still managed to look as if she was ready for a fashion shoot. Connor could never understand how she did it.

'Who's next?' asked Toby, coming over to join them. The small dark-haired boy was the Tigers' APL. He was fiddling with the complicated-looking watch on his wrist. 'I'm not sure if my altimeter is working properly.'

'Don't worry,' laughed Connor. 'James has got a machine that logs the whole flight. We went up to four thousand feet. I reckon I could see for a hundred kilometres. And anyway, you need to look out for birds rather than checking your watch.'

'Birds?' said Toby. 'Why?'

'The birds know how to find the warm air,' Connor explained. 'The thermals, remember? Julie told us about them but I'd forgotten until James reminded me.'

'I want to find one,' Andy said. 'I'm going to strap my camcorder to my arm and video everything I see. Do you think you can see Wales from up there? That's where my family came from,' he reminded the others. 'They lived in this really remote valley. My parents keep promising we can go there, but somehow it never happens.'

'Maybe you can,' said Julie, who had been listening to their conversation. 'You know you're all going to be planning an expedition this term? There's no reason why you couldn't go to Wales.'

'It's a long way,' said Toby. 'How would we get there?'

'That's easy,' said Jay enthusiastically. 'We could cycle. I've always wanted to go on a long trip on my bike.'

Andy looked at Julie. 'We couldn't . . . could we?'

'I don't see why not,' she replied as Connor remembered the blue line of mountains he'd glimpsed from the paraglider. 'You probably wouldn't be able to cycle the whole way, but you could take your bikes on the train for some of it.

It would fit in well with what Rick and I had planned. Next weekend we're going on our night hike, but our first meeting after that will be about cycle maintenance. Hey – look! Abby's about to land.'

They all stood up to watch as James and Abby touched down and stumbled towards them.

'That was just incredible!' Abby gasped as James helped her to remove her harness. 'It was totally amazing! Really awesome! I want to do it again.'

Priya sat and listened as Abby described her ascent and the other Tigers filled her in on the possible expedition to Wales.

'We might have to do a few repairs to our bikes first,' Abby said. 'I'm pretty sure mine's got a flat tyre.'

'It'll be OK,' said Jay. 'I can help you fix it. You can go a really long way on a bike in a day. They cover hundreds of kilometres in the Tour de France.'

'Yeah,' said Toby, laughing. 'But we're not in the Tour de France, are we?'

'I wouldn't mind, one day . . .' Jay said, then looked embarrassed.

Priya glanced at him curiously. She and Jay had joined the Scouts on the same day the previous year, and she was still learning new things about the stocky fair-haired boy. Jay had been a reluctant Scout at first, and although Priya knew that he liked cycling and owned a shiny, expensive mountain bike, she would never have guessed that he was ambitious to become a serious racer.

The others had all started talking about the night hike that Julie had mentioned. Since their winter adventure in the snow the Scouts had been busy with a series of indoor activities and as a result she now had an Artist badge and a Chef badge newly sewn onto her uniform. But now, for the first time since Priya had joined the Scouts, they were planning an activity that she really didn't want to do. The thought of stumbling about in the countryside at night gave her the creeps. She was a bit worried about this cycling idea too, because she didn't even own a bike. Maybe Mihir would lend her his. He hadn't ridden it for ages. She would ask him when she got home—

'Hey, Priya!' Abby's friendly voice interrupted her thoughts. 'You need to get ready. Here comes Andy.'

Priya stood up and walked over to the landing zone. Connor joined her, his blond hair still messed up from his flight. His blue eyes were screwed up against the sun.

'Hey – good luck! It's an incredible rush – a bit scary at first, but you'll see, it's amazing to be able to fly.'

'Thanks,' said Priya quietly. She could tell that Connor was doing his Patrol Leader thing and trying to put her at ease. She smiled at him gratefully.

They both watched as James came towards them.

'Great!' he said. 'You don't look like you weigh much. We should be able to go really high.'

Priya listened carefully as he strapped her in and gave her some final instructions. 'Ready?' he asked her. 'Run!'

Priya felt her heart race as she ran with him, then suddenly the paraglider soared into the air. She felt a rush of elation as the earth seemed to shrink below her and the air rushed past her ears. As they glided out across the valley, she remembered what Connor had said earlier about looking out for birds.

'Would you like to try steering?' asked James in her ear.

'Really?' She couldn't believe he was offering.

'Sure. It's easy. Reach up and take the controls. That's it. Keep your hands level.'

Priya could feel the wind on the wing, trembling through the web of cords that ended in the hand-grips. It was alive!

'That's great! You're a natural. Let's steer to

the left. Look to the left. Left hand down, right hand up. Gently does it. Brilliant!'

The paraglider swooped round in a wide circle and began to climb slowly. More and more hills came into view. And then Priya saw the birds. 'Look!' She almost took her hand off the controls in her eagerness, and the wing gave a sudden lurch.

'Whoa! Hang on there!' James took back the controls.

'Sorry, James. But I saw some swifts.' Priya gazed all around, trying to spot the flock of birds. 'There!' She pointed.

'Hey, cool!' said James, swinging them round once more. 'Let's go!'

As they met the rising air of the thermal, Priya felt the paraglider accelerate upwards, turning tightly. Up, and up, and up. The wind was cold on her face, but she hardly felt it as the ground receded below them and she saw the long line of distant hills that Connor had seen before her. Wales! It looked magical. It would be so great to go there.

As they turned once more and she picked out the two tiny white dots that were the Scout minibuses far, far below, she decided that there was no way Mihir wasn't going to lend her his bike.

Just let him try and stop her!

CHAPTER 2

'Well, at least one of us has a decent bike,' Connor said as Jay rode up to Scout HQ on a Friday evening two weeks later on a gleaming mountain bike that looked as if it had never seen a speck of dirt.

'Well, well,' murmured Connor's dad appreciatively. Dr Sutcliff was a GP at the local health centre; he helped out with the Scouts whenever he could. 'That's a lovely machine,' he continued. 'Expensive, I should think. And you look after it – unlike Connor!'

'Dad, that's not fair!' Connor replied hotly, before realizing that his dad was smiling. 'My bike's got a puncture, that's all,' he told Jay.

'So has Toby's,' observed Dr Sutcliff.

Toby's bike was also making a scraping sound

as he wheeled it along. Toby shook his head as he approached the others. 'I don't know why it's making that noise,' he said. 'Maybe I'll have to get a new bike.'

'You might not be the only one,' said Connor, looking over to where Priya's dad was lifting a bicycle out of the back of his car.

Mr Gupta walked over to join them. The bike rattled and clanked as he pushed it along. Both its tyres were flat and one of them looked as if something had tried to eat it.

'It used to be my brother's,' Priya said apologetically. 'I've never really done much cycling.'

'I think it might have been a nice bike once,' said Jay.

'It was,' Mr Gupta told him. 'It cost me a lot of money. But Mihir decided he was too old to be riding around on a bicycle.' Priya's elder brother was sixteen, and very friendly with Connor's sister, Ellie.

'I told him if he wasn't using it he had to lend

it to me,' said Priya. 'Only I didn't think it would be quite this bad.'

'I asked the chap at the bike shop to tell me what parts I needed.' Mr Gupta held up a large carrier bag to show Connor. 'I've brought them along. Priya says one of you is an expert and you have to fix the bikes yourselves to get your badges.'

'That's right,' agreed Connor. 'But it's Jay who's the expert, not me.'

Jay shuffled his feet and his neck reddened. 'I'm not really an expert,' he mumbled. 'I just like bikes, that's all. What have you got there?'

He peered into Mr Gupta's bag and then inspected the bike carefully. 'It's not quite as bad as it looks,' he said finally. 'I bet we can fix it.'

'I hope you can fix ours too.' Andy skidded to a halt beside Abby. Connor was pleased to see that at least two members of Tiger Patrol had bikes that could actually be ridden. 'My brakes are rubbish,' Andy went on. 'I have to use my feet to help me stop.'

'And I've only got one gear,' said Abby. 'I think I'm supposed to have fifteen – or eighteen. I'm not sure.'

'What do you think, Jay?' asked Connor. 'If we're going on this expedition we have to show Rick and Julie that we can fix our own bikes.'

All the Tigers were looking expectantly at Jay. His face broke into a grin. 'Bikes aren't complicated,' he said. 'I've got my tools here, and Rick and Julie have got plenty more over there. It'll be fine. Let's get started.'

'Don't worry. I'll show you what to do,' Jay said to Priya as she contemplated the array of parts that were spread out on the ground. 'Connor and Toby can fix their own punctures and then they can help the others.'

'I thought I had to do everything myself,' Priya said.

'I've been checking,' Connor told her, looking up from his flat tyre. 'You have to look after your bike and keep it in good condition for six months. You have to know *how* to do lots of things, but there's plenty of time for all that later.'

'You won't have any trouble,' said Jay. 'It's easy. We'll put the new tyre and inner tube on the back wheel together, then you can do the front one while I fit the gears.'

Jay was a patient teacher. He showed Priya how to inflate the inner tube just a little before starting to work the bead of the tyre over the wheel rim. He made it look easy, but when Priya tried, she thought her thumbs would fall off before the final section of tyre finally popped into place.

'Now make sure that you haven't caught the tube anywhere . . .' Jay showed her how to check. 'OK, cool. Now pump it up.'

Priya stared at the pump that he had brought with him. It stood on the ground and had a handle you pressed down. She couldn't figure out how the little tube attached to the valve, but again, Jay showed her.

'Just push it on hard and snap this lever down,'

he said. 'It just holds it in place. It looks complicated, but it pumps really well. These tyres should be inflated to seventy psi. You'd never do that with an ordinary pump.'

'Wow!' exclaimed Priya, feeling the tyre when she'd finished. 'It's like a rock.'

Jay took the wheel from her. 'Most people ride around on tyres that are far too soft,' he said. 'That's why they get punctures and their tyres wear out fast. You do the other wheel and I'll fit the new gears onto this one. I'll have to take it into the workshop and put it in the vice.'

Priya would have liked to watch Jay working on her wheel. It would be great if she could learn to do everything the way he did. But right now she needed to remember how to do this other tyre without him to help her. She cleaned out the wheel rim and fitted the new rim-tape, then began to put the tyre in place. It was hard work, and she'd only just finished when Jay returned. She looked up and saw that all the other Tigers were watching her.

'That's fantastic, Priya,' said Abby.

'I *like* doing this,' she replied. 'Maybe I'll become a bike mechanic.'

'But then you'd mess up all those amazing clothes you wear,' laughed Abby. Priya stuck her tongue out playfully.

Jay checked Priya's work and nodded. 'Great job,' he said. 'I'll just finish the gears.'

Priya watched, fascinated, as Jay removed the large cogs that were powered by the pedals and replaced them with the new ones her dad had bought. Andy had taken out his camcorder and was filming everything Jay did: he fitted the back wheel into the frame, and fixed the new chain in place; then he ran the chain over the gears and made some final adjustments.

'That's it,' he said, turning the bike the right way up. 'It's ready to ride.'

Priya put on her helmet then got on the bike and rode unsteadily around the car park. The bike felt huge, and she had to reassure herself from time to time by putting her feet down on the ground. But she made it back to the others without falling off.

'How does it feel?' asked Jay.

'Big,' said Priya. 'And I don't really know how to change gear. My old bike didn't have any gears at all.'

'Don't worry,' said Connor encouragingly. 'You'll soon get used to it.'

'You'll have to,' Abby told her. 'Look. Rick's setting up an obstacle course. I think we're going to have races.'

Priya wobbled off on another circuit of the tarmac, gradually feeling more confident on her bike. Jay gave her a wave and she took one hand off the handlebars and waved back.

Andy looked up and saw her. 'Hey, Priya,' he called. 'Come and look at these.'

The Tigers had all gathered around him and were looking excitedly at the photos in his hands. 'I took these on the night hike last week,' he told Priya. 'It's a shame you couldn't come, but at least you can see what it was like.'

He held out a photo of four smiling Tigers, all with head-torches gleaming on their foreheads, lighting each other's faces. Behind them, everything was black. Priya suppressed a shudder as Andy explained what they'd done. 'It was much easier than when we were on the moors, or out in that snowstorm,' he said. 'All we had to do was follow paths and make sure we didn't take any wrong turns.'

'And with Toby and Jay doing most of the navigating we didn't have to worry about a thing,' added Abby. 'We had a great time.'

'In fact, Abby was the only problem,' said Andy. 'She did her usual thing, charging on ahead and not waiting for anyone.'

'Until she met a cow,' said Connor, laughing. 'She thought it was a bull and came running back like an Olympic sprinter.'

'I did not,' Abby retorted. 'I mean, I never thought it was a bull, but even a cow is pretty scary if it suddenly appears out of the darkness. Actually, there were lots of cows, but they were all lying down and they didn't bother us at all. We just walked round them.'

Andy found a photo of the cows, lit up by the head-torches. Priya thought it looked creepy. She had pretended to be ill on the evening of the night hike, and had been feeling bad about that. But now she saw the photos she knew she'd been right. She would have hated it.

'Great photos, Andy,' said Rick, the Scout Leader, looking over Andy's shoulder. 'Let's take a look at these bikes.'

The Tigers stood back while he inspected their work. When he was finished he stood up again. 'Well done, all of you. Connor, you should be proud of your patrol.'

'Well, actually, we could never have done it without Jay,' Connor admitted. 'I think he could probably build a bike from scratch.'

Jay looked embarrassed once again, but pleased at the same time.

Rick gave him an approving look. 'That's great,' he said. 'It looks like you're actually going to be ready to take on the Expedition Challenge at half-term. You should start thinking about it now.'

'Julie said we could go to Wales. Is that really true?' Andy sounded excited.

'I don't see why not,' Rick said, smiling. 'I was very impressed by how well you did at the paragliding, and on the night hike. It's a shame you missed it, Priya. Are you feeling better?'

Priya nodded guiltily. She hated pretending.

But Rick was still talking. 'You'll need to plan your expedition very carefully, but I'm sure you can manage that. By the time we've completed all our biking activities you should be very competent cyclists. Next week we've got road-sense training, and in two weeks' time we'll be going to a mountain-biking event on the moors.'

'Yes!' the Tigers exclaimed in unison.

'But my bike isn't a mountain bike,' said Abby after a moment.

'Doesn't matter,' Rick told her. 'You can hire them quite cheaply. Take a break for five minutes, then we'll try my obstacle courses. You might even want to practise. It looks like Guy is a bit of an expert.'

Guy from Wolf Patrol had brought a tiny BMX bike as well as his mountain bike and was riding around with the front wheel high in the air.

'No worries,' laughed Jay, leaping onto his bike. 'We can do that too – right, Toby?'

'Just about,' Toby agreed, a little uncertainly, as he mounted his own bike. 'Jay showed me the other day,' he told the others. 'I'm not too good at it yet.'

Priya watched as the two boys rode around. Toby managed to get up on one wheel for a few moments, his face a mask of concentration. Jay was just amazing. He rode right across the car park on his back wheel, jumped his bike up onto the steps outside the entrance to Scout HQ and then rode all the way back the same way. He stopped in front of the Tigers, balanced on his back wheel.

Priya clapped her hands. 'How do you do that?' she asked.

'Practice,' said Jay. 'Plus I just love riding bikes. Hey, Toby, that's cool!'

Toby was balancing on his back wheel, spinning round in a circle. His front wheel came down with a thud and his bike toppled over. 'I haven't quite perfected it yet,' he said with a serious expression as the others laughed.

Andy and Abby had started discussing the expedition again.

'What exactly *is* the Expedition Challenge?' Priya asked them. 'I mean, I know you all want to go to Wales, but where will we stay when we get there? Will there be a hostel or something?'

'We camp, of course,' said Andy. 'And I bet we'll be able to camp somewhere really wild.'

'And we do it on our own,' said Abby. 'No grown-ups. I mean, we have to check in, and someone might camp near by and make sure that we've arrived safely, but we do the whole journey on our own. Imagine sleeping in a tiny tent, miles from anywhere. You'll love it, Priya!'

Priya nodded and tried to smile. She told herself that she was being stupid. The expedition was only one thing in a whole lot of activities that Rick and Julie had planned. She wasn't scared of riding a bike on the road, even though she'd never done it before. And she wasn't scared of the mountain-bike trail. That sounded really exciting. The trouble was, she kept imagining what it was going to be like sleeping in a small tent miles from anywhere. She suddenly wished she hadn't secretly watched her brother's horror films. Who knew what might be lurking in the shadows?

She decided that there was no way she would go on the expedition.

CHAPTER 3

On the morning of the mountain-bike event Priya discovered that her whole family were planning to come and watch. 'You can't!' she said. 'You know I won't be any good.'

'What nonsense,' her mum said. 'Look at how quickly you learned to ski. I know what you're like. You'll just keep at it until you can do it.'

'No, Priya's right,' said Mihir as he helped his sister load her bike into the car. 'I'm coming along so I can watch her fall off in the mud.'

Priya gave him her best withering look but it only made his grin wider. She knew how much he loved to wind her up.

When they finally arrived at the mountain-bike centre, there seemed to be hundreds of Scouts milling around in the car park, and people

were unloading bikes from vehicles of every shape and size. Priya spotted Connor, Andy and Abby standing around with their bikes. A few minutes later Jay arrived with Toby. They were both looking very hot.

'We cycled all the way,' Toby said proudly as he took off his helmet.

'And most of it's uphill,' said Jay. 'I need a drink.'

'Will you still have energy left for more cycling?' asked Abby.

'Of course we will.' Toby was small, wiry and very fit.

Priya saw that Toby had fitted a carrier frame to his bike and was now searching in the rucksack that was strapped to it. She knew that he could always be relied on to bring his enormous rucksack, which was filled with the most extraordinary things. This time he pulled out a whole handful of chocolate nut bars.

'Here,' he said. 'Does anyone want one?'

As he handed them out, Abby couldn't resist

teasing him. 'One day you're actually going to bring out a kitchen sink, and I don't think I'll even be surprised.'

Priya laughed along with everyone else as she reached out for a bar.

'Well, actually' – Toby started digging around in his rucksack – 'I do have something that could be used as a kitche—'

'All right, everyone, gather round,' said Rick. 'We're all going to ride round the Curlew Trail.'

'I'll show you the kitchen sink I have later,' whispered Toby, smiling at the bemused faces of the other Tigers.

Rick continued: 'The Curlew Trail is waymarked so there's no danger of you getting lost. Not even if you're Tiger Patrol!'

'We never actually got lost,' said Andy, pulling a funny face at the others. 'We just took a different route!'

Priya caught the twinkle in his eye and laughed, thinking back to the Orienteering Challenge that the patrol undertook last year. It had been her first expedition and the 'different route' had been a little scary at the time. She was glad they had pulled through as a team. She looked down at the badge on her sleeve. It had been her first one and she was very proud of it.

She turned her attention back to Rick. 'The point is,' he continued, 'you're to use that trail and no other.'

'But isn't it a bit easy, Rick?' asked Ben from Eagle Patrol, who was a keen mountain biker.

'Don't worry, Ben,' Rick said. 'When we've all completed the course we have some proper racing planned. We'll have heats to select a representative from each troop – so each patrol needs to choose one rider – and at the end of the day one person will be the champion. They've set up a really challenging course for the races.'

The Tigers exchanged glances. 'It has to be you, Jay,' Connor whispered. 'You'll do it, won't you?'

The others all nodded their agreement. Jay

had been fastest through the obstacle course and he'd been brilliant in the training.

He looked around at everyone, clearly pleased. 'Thanks,' he said. 'I've always wanted to race here. Their courses are awesome.'

Rick was still talking. 'The Curlew Trail is twelve kilometres and it's got some steepish hills, as you can see from the maps Julie is handing round. If you can do it in an hour and a half you'll be doing very well. I suggest you tackle this in pairs. If you make your way to the start, they'll set you off. They'll give everyone a time at the end.'

'I'm going to go at the back with Priya,' Connor told the others. 'We'll take it slowly – we don't want to get in the way of people who want to go fast.'

'Like me and Toby,' said Jay. 'And I bet Andy and Abby will be quick too. You're not going to stop and take pictures, are you, Andy?'

Andy had taken his camcorder out of its case and was filming the other Scouts as they prepared

33

to set off. 'Not today,' he replied, grinning. 'Let's have a race. Me and Abby against you and Toby.'

Priya watched as Andy and Abby put on their helmets and sped off after the others. Moments later, Toby and Jay were pedalling off along the first, flat section of the trail and into a group of trees. Shortly afterwards they emerged higher up the hillside, both standing up on their pedals, climbing rapidly upwards.

'It looks hard,' Priya said.

'That's only because they're trying to go fast,' replied Connor. 'We'll go up slowly in a low gear. Don't worry, you'll be fine.'

Andy and Abby seemed to be racing each other to the top. They were riding side by side, and as they crested the hill, Abby made contact with Andy's bike. Just for a second it seemed certain that Andy would fall. He wobbled comically, then righted the bike and cycled off in pursuit of his friend.

'Phew!' said Connor. 'If they get round

without crashing it'll be a miracle. Come on, Priya. We'd better get ready.'

Priya took a deep breath and followed him to the start line.

They were the last pair to set off, and Connor could see that Priya was unsteady. She was probably nervous. The track was wide at first and the surface was smooth, but as soon as they were out of sight of the start, they turned into a small wood and the ground became bumpy with tree roots. Priya slowed down at once.

'Try to keep going,' Connor said. 'The faster you ride over this stuff, the easier it is. You go ahead of me.'

He was glad to see the determined set of Priya's jaw as she speeded up slightly and rattled over the lumpy ground. The trail turned to the right and began to climb.

'Change down,' called Connor. 'You need a low gear!'

But it was too late. Priya had almost stopped

moving when she tried to click down through the gears. There was a grinding clatter and then she stopped. Connor pulled up beside her. 'What happened?' she asked. 'I don't understand.'

'The gears won't work if you're not moving. You have to think ahead. I should have warned you sooner. Here – hold your bike still.'

Connor lifted the back end of Priya's bike while she held the handlebars, then reached forward and turned the pedals, and the chain clicked over onto the largest cog on the back wheel. 'There,' he said. 'Now you're in low gear. You'll be able to pedal up the hill now.'

Priya shook her head, her brown eyes filling with tears. 'I'm sorry, Connor. I'm going to mess it up for everyone.'

'It's not a race,' said Connor, fixing her with a brilliant smile, trying his best to encourage her. 'You'll get better at it. Go on, I'm right behind you.'

He stood on his pedals and caught up with her

as they came over the brow of the hill. Heathery moors stretched away into the distance. The next part of the trail followed a track that had grass growing down the middle, so that it looked like two paths side by side. It curved away across the moor, and they could see the boy who had started before them, a surprisingly long way ahead.

'OK,' said Priya. 'I can manage this all right. Let's try and catch up.' Not waiting for Connor, she set off quickly, changing up through her gears.

'Priya, wait!' called Connor. 'Slow down!'

But Priya was gone. Connor jumped onto his bike and chased after her. The track was smooth enough here, but he knew that there would be surprises in store. Still, he thought, at the moment Priya seemed to be doing really well. And she carried on doing well, surprising Connor with her speed and balance as they reached the halfway point on the course and plunged down off the open moorland, following a rocky track beneath overhanging oak and birch trees.

'Take it easy down here,' Connor said. 'Keep your brakes on.'

'Don't worry!' Priya replied. 'I've got the hang of this now.'

She released her brakes and hurtled down the twisting track. As Connor followed, she disappeared from view round a bend and there was a sudden loud yell.

'Priya!' Connor yelled urgently. 'Priya, are you OK?'

As soon as he turned the corner, he saw a shaken-looking Priya coming up a slope towards him, pushing her bike between the young trees that covered the hillside. 'It's OK,' she said in an unsteady voice. 'I couldn't make the turn so I carried on down there and I managed to stop. I did fall off though.'

'I can see that,' Connor said, laughing with relief. Priya was covered in mud from head to foot.

'I'm glad you think it's funny,' she said crossly.

'I don't,' he replied, forcing himself to keep a straight face. 'But if you could see what you look like . . .'

But Priya wasn't looking at Connor. She was inspecting the ground at her feet. 'Look!' she exclaimed. 'It's not just me who came off here. Someone else did too.'

'I bet it was Abby,' said Connor.

'Well, whoever it was,' said Priya. 'They didn't come back up again like I did. I think we should go and take a look.'

Connor leaned his bike against a tree and bent to inspect the tracks in the mud. 'You're right,' he said. 'If they are still down there, they'll be easy enough to find.'

'Be careful,' warned Priya as he made his way down the muddy slope, lurching from tree to tree. 'It gets very steep.'

'There *is* someone,' yelled Connor suddenly. 'Can you see? Just down there.' He pointed between the trees.

A Scout was lying underneath his bike. When

he saw Connor, he called out weakly: 'Help! Over here.'

Connor and Priya quickly scrambled down to join him, and Connor lifted the bike carefully off the pale-faced boy. There was a gash on his forehead and blood was trickling down the side of his face. 'I've done something to my leg,' he told them. 'I tried to get up, but I couldn't.'

'Don't worry,' replied Connor. 'We'll fetch help. Priya, you'd better go. Be as quick as you can. Rick said the second half of the course is faster, so you'd better just carry on the way we were going. It's thanks to Priya we found you,' he told the boy.

'What's your name and your troop?' Priya asked. 'They'll be worried about you.'

'Steve Brewster. First Matfield.' He winced and groaned. 'I'm so glad you found me. I was beginning to think I'd be stuck here for ever.'

Priya raced off up the hill.

CHAPTER 4

Priya leaped onto her bike and continued down the rocky track as fast as she dared, saying the boy's name over and over to herself so that she wouldn't forget. *Steve Brewster. Steve Brewster.* It was obvious that he was badly hurt. That cut on his head had looked really nasty. And she'd seen the worried look in Connor's eyes.

Her front wheel hit a rock and the shock jarred down her arms as she fought to control the bike. She bounced off a tree root, and for a moment she was in the air. The bike slammed onto the ground again and the back wheel skidded beneath her, but she twisted the handlebars and put a foot down for an instant, and she was off again, splashing though a little stream and then climbing steeply, her legs burning with the effort, until she came out on the open moor again.

The track snaked away under the hot sun. Priya shifted up through the gears until she was racing across the hillside in the highest one. She began to pass other cyclists, but she paid them no attention. She zigzagged down into another, much bigger valley, and crossed a wide, rocky river. As she neared the end of the trail she began to pass more and more riders, most of them muddy and sweating. The final stretch was a straight smooth path that ran through the trees back to the centre. Her tyres hissed on the tarmac and she felt as if her lungs were bursting as she crossed the finish line to a chorus of cheers. The other members of Tiger Patrol gathered around her, patting her on the back as she took long, ragged breaths.

'Incredible!' said Abby. Or at least Priya thought it was Abby. The girl who had spoken had wet hair plastered over a face that was streaked with mud. 'You must have overtaken at least twenty people. But where's Connor?'

'No,' gasped Priya, finally able to speak. 'You don't understand. We found this boy who'd crashed. Steve Brewster from the First Matfield. I have to tell someone. Connor stayed with him, but Steve has hurt himself badly.'

Instantly Toby ran off towards the organizers' tent at the edge of the car park. Priya's legs suddenly turned to jelly, and Abby grabbed her before she could fall, and lowered her gently to the ground. Seconds later, Toby came running back, with Rick and an anxious-looking Scout Leader from the First Matfield close behind him.

'How is he?' asked the Scout Leader, whose name was Craig.

'He's banged his head,' replied Priya. 'And he's hurt his leg. Connor thought we shouldn't move him.'

'Good stuff,' said Craig. 'Can you show me exactly where they are?'

He held out a map and Priya looked at it carefully, knowing how important it was not to make a mistake. 'We'd just come off this moorland here . . .' she said, pointing at the place on the map. 'And we were coming down this steep track here . . . Yes! That's the place. The track turns sharply to the right and I went straight on. I was going too fast but I managed to stop. Steve must have just kept on going. He's there.' She pointed again.

'Excellent, Priya,' Rick said as a quad bike drew up beside them with two green-suited para-medics aboard. The Scout Leaders briefed them quickly, pointing out the place on the map, and the quad bike took off up the track.

'There's nothing more we can do at the moment,' Rick said as they watched the last stragglers riding up to the finish. 'Well done again, Priya. If you can ride as fast as that, then maybe *you* should ride in the race!' He paused and surveyed the group. 'You know, I'm not sure who's the muddiest of you lot.'

'Am I really that bad?' asked Priya as Rick walked away.

'Wait,' said Toby. 'I'll show you.'

'You're completely crazy,' Andy said to him as he pulled a small plastic mirror out of his pack. 'Why have you got that?'

'Mirrors have all sorts of uses,' replied Toby seriously. 'For instance, you could use this for signalling if you got lost on the moors.'

Andy blinked as Toby flashed a bright circle of sunlight across his face. The others laughed.

'Take a look,' Toby told Priya, holding the mirror in front of her.

She hardly recognized her own face. She had been so intent on riding fast that she hadn't noticed the chalky spray thrown up by the bikes she had overtaken. She was covered in blotchy white spots that seemed to glow on her dark skin. Bits of grass and leaves were caught in her hair.

'And you're normally the best dressed of us all,' laughed Abby.

'It was worth it,' replied Priya. 'That boy was in a lot of pain. And there's no way I'm riding in a race, by the way. I'm not even sure I've got the energy to walk.'

'I bet you'll be able to make it over to the barbecue,' said Jay, grinning. 'They've got excellent hot dogs over there.'

As soon as Jay said it, Priya realized that she was starving, and the Tigers made their way over to the barbecue. They were all eating hot dogs and burgers when they saw the quad bike returning, with the injured Scout strapped to a stretcher on the back. The quad bike was moving very slowly so as not to jar him, and Connor was riding behind them on his bike.

An ambulance had pulled up on the far side of the car park and the paramedics stopped beside it. Connor waved Priya over to join them.

'Excellent directions, young lady,' said one of the paramedics. 'We found him very quickly, thanks to you, and you'll be glad to know that he's going to be absolutely fine.'

Steve grinned woozily up from the stretcher. 'You're so beautiful . . .' he slurred, then closed his eyes. Priya felt herself blushing and was glad of the mud covering her face.

'Don't worry,' laughed the paramedic. 'We gave him something for the pain and it's gone to his head! We'd better get him off to the hospital. Enjoy the rest of your day, you two. I reckon you've earned it.'

'OK,' said Connor as the ambulance drove away. 'Show me these hot dogs. Is Jay ready for the race?'

All the Scouts from the Sixth Matfield Troop were standing together, with Rick and Julie behind them.

'Can he do it?' asked Sajiv, the Panthers' PL. 'He looks really nervous.'

All six finalists were lined up at the start, having been selected from earlier heats.

'We're going to find out,' said Connor, looking at the grim set of Jay's jaw as he waited for the signal. 'Here they go.'

Connor felt confident that Jay could win this;

after all, he'd won their troop heat easily. But he knew that a boy from the First Matfield, Jez, was also very good.

The starter's whistle blew and the six bikes sped away down the track. Within seconds two bikes were clearly ahead of the rest – Jez and Jay racing furiously side by side. Connor watched as the lead racers started to climb a series of steep hairpins towards the top of the hill.

'There's a narrow point coming up on the track,' said Abby, standing next to Connor. 'One of them's going to have to let the other one go ahead.'

'It's like a game of chicken,' murmured Toby.

'But I don't think either of them is going to give way,' said Connor.

The point where the track narrowed and turned more steeply uphill was now just metres away.

'It's no good,' said Andy, who was filming everything. 'They'll crash.'

Connor watched with his heart in his mouth

as the two cyclists came together. The boy in the red helmet veered off the track for a moment, but then clawed his way back on course. The Tigers all groaned – and then gasped as they saw Jay careering wildly over rocks and grass before finally regaining the track.

'He did it!' cried Priya. 'Oh, well done, Jay.'

'He stayed on his bike,' said Toby gloomily. 'But he's ten metres behind now. It's over – Jay'll never win now.'

CHAPTER 5

A silence fell over the watching crowd as the last of the finalists disappeared over the top of the hill.

'What do you think?' asked Priya. 'Can he do it?'

'He'll do his best,' replied Connor. 'That's for sure.'

Connor was amazed how much he'd come to like and respect Jay. There had been a time when Jay had first joined the Scouts when he hadn't been sure if they would get along. Connor looked down at his watch. A minute had gone by already. Beside him, Abby was chewing her fingers, while Andy had his camcorder focused unmovingly on the notch in the hillside where the riders would reappear. Toby's eyes were also on his watch as the seconds ticked by.

'Come on, Jay,' muttered Priya. 'We want to see you come over that hill in the lead.'

'Two minutes thirty!' said Connor.

'There!' yelled Toby, and then there was a groan from the Sixth Matfield supporters as they saw Jez's red helmet.

'Jay's still behind,' said Abby.

'But not by much,' said Andy through gritted teeth. 'Come on, Jay, you can still make it!'

All the spectators were yelling now – some for Jez, but far more, Connor realized, for Jay. And Jay was right on the other boy's back wheel as they rode, at reckless, tearing speed, down the rocky path. First Jez was airborne, and a split second behind him Jay took off. For a long moment both bikes were in the air.

'This is going to be just awesome in slow motion,' breathed Andy, his eye still glued to the viewfinder of his camcorder.

There was a gasp from the watchers as both bikes landed together, side by side.

'He can do it,' gasped Priya. 'He's going to get past!'

'No,' said Connor, shaking his head. 'Jez has got the inside line round that bend – look!'

Sure enough, as the path made a hairpin bend, Jez managed to force Jay to the side so that there was no room to pass.

'That's it, then,' said Abby. 'There's nothing more he can do.'

'Wait,' said Connor. 'What's he doing? He's crazy!'

There was one final bend before the straight race to the finish. A short way before it the trail divided, and a very narrow side path led sharply upwards before finishing above a sheer two-metre drop. Jay had pointed it out to Connor earlier. 'You can go over it,' he'd said. 'I've seen people do it. You have to get the landing just right – hit the ground at the right point on the slope – a bit like ski-jumping.'

'Don't even think about it,' Connor had told him. 'It's not worth it.'

Connor saw Jez glance behind him. His bike wobbled for a second as he realized that Jay wasn't where he expected him to be. Then he looked up, and at that moment Jay came flying over the edge of the little cliff. His bike went unbelievably high, and Connor saw that he was fighting to keep the wheels in line and hold the bike at the right angle, his face a grim mask of concentration. He landed in a spray of dirt and pebbles – three metres ahead of Jez.

A huge cheer went up from the watching crowd, and the Tigers were jumping up and down with excitement as Jay sprinted to the finish and crossed the line a clear three metres ahead of his rival.

The Tigers reached him just as Jez was shaking his hand. 'Unbelievable!' he said. 'I thought I'd won it. That was the last thing I expected you to do. You should join our club, you know. We race all over the country.'

Jay's face was beaming as the Tigers exchanged high-fives with him.

'Well now,' said Rick, approaching them, serious-faced, 'that was a very risky manoeuvre, young Jay.'

Jay's face fell and they all turned towards Rick, whose face suddenly cracked into a huge smile.

'Very risky, but you executed it perfectly. With all the skills I've seen on show here today, I'm sure that you lot are ready to go for your Expedition Challenge. You can start planning it just as soon as you like. Oh, and by the way – that lad you rescued is going to be fine. He was asking after you, Priya, I hear.'

Priya blushed amid the laughter of the other Tigers. She smiled, but a little later, as the others moved back to the barbecue, excitedly discussing the prospect of a real expedition, Connor noticed her biting her lip. She'd had a great day, but he could see that something was still bothering her. He was about to ask her what it was when Andy said: 'That's right, isn't it, Connor? We're completely on our own?'

He was drawn into the conversation, and the

next time he looked at Priya she was laughing happily with her parents.

I must have imagined it, he thought.

Priya had noticed Connor looking at her strangely. She hoped he'd thought she was just embarrassed about Steve asking after her. Anything was better than having him think she wasn't ready to go on this expedition.

Toby was talking about it now. 'Julie said we could get to Wales on the train,' he said. 'But is that where everyone wants to go? We ought to take a vote before we decide.'

'Well, I *really* want to go there,' Andy said, and Priya was surprised by the passion in his voice. 'My grandfather grew up in a valley right in the middle of Wales, and I've never been there. All the roads are very small, and I bet there's not much traffic. And the best thing of all is that there's a campsite right in the valley. It's very small and simple. I looked it up on the Internet and it sounds perfect.'

'We saw Wales from the paragliders,' Connor said. 'At least, some of us did.' He aimed a mischievous smile at Abby and Andy. They knew that he and Priya had gone far higher than any of the others.

'We can get most of the way on the train,' Andy said excitedly. 'I checked. It only takes two hours.'

'It looks like that's where we're going, then,' said Toby, smiling. 'What do we have to do next?'

Priya listened as the others began to discuss Andy's plan. He seemed to have done a lot of research and was starting to describe his grandfather's valley when Connor interrupted him.

'We have to persuade an adult to shadow us first,' he said. 'They don't actually go on the expedition. Just stay nearby and check that we arrive safely. It really will be like doing it on our own.'

Andy frowned. 'My dad's going to be away filming,' he said. 'He wouldn't be able to do it.' Andy's dad was a cameraman with the local TV station and he was sometimes away for weeks at a time. The others all looked equally doubtful.

'Don't worry,' Connor said. 'I bet my dad will be able to do it. And if he can't, my grandpa would definitely be up for it.'

They all laughed. Connor's grandpa was a legendary ex-Scout.

Priya could feel her hands getting sweaty and she shivered, despite the heat of the sun. She was angry with herself. It was so stupid, being scared, but the fact was, it was giving her nightmares that woke her, terrified, in the middle of the night. She wanted to go on the expedition, she really did. But she didn't want to sleep in a tent in the darkness.

Ten minutes later, Priya left her friends and went over to join her family by the car. She saw Jay exchanging phone numbers with Jez. He gave her a cheerful wave.

'He was brilliant, wasn't he?' said Priya's mum as her dad fetched a plastic sheet and stowed her dripping bike away in the back of the car.

'And you are incredibly muddy,' said Mihir. 'I think you look better like that.'

'Pay no attention,' said Mrs Gupta. 'You were amazing. You all were.' And she gave Priya a big kiss.

'Right then,' Priya's dad said. 'Let's get you home. I bet you're looking forward to a hot bath.'

They drove out of the car park, past groups of muddy Scouts putting equally muddy bikes into cars and vans.

'You're very quiet,' Mr Gupta said with a sideways glance at his daughter. Priya didn't reply, and he drove on for a while in silence. 'You've certainly learned how to ride a bike,' he said finally. 'I was very impressed.'

Priya forced a smile. 'Thanks. I'm just a bit tired, that's all.'

'You must be,' he replied. 'This was your first attempt though, so it's only natural that it is a bit tough. By the time you go on the bigger expedition, you'll feel much better, you'll see.'

Priya hoped her dad was right.

CHAPTER 6

It was a week later, and the Tigers were sitting on the grass outside Scout HQ. They were buzzing with excitement. Rick and Julie had given them the final go-ahead to try for the Expedition Challenge.

'I've got all the train timetables here,' Andy said. 'I went to the station last night.'

'And I've got the maps,' added Toby.

'I downloaded all the details about the campsite,' Connor said. 'We can look at that later. First we have to make a list. Each train we're going to catch, where we change, when we arrive. Then we have to work out estimates for when we'll arrive at each place on our journey.'

The Tigers set to work.

'We ought to leave early in the morning,' Toby

59

said, looking up from the timetable. 'I know we *could* ride the forty kilometres to the campsite in a couple of hours, but it would be hard work and we wouldn't have time to look at anything on the way. So let's say it'll take four hours.'

'That's about right,' agreed Connor. 'There are mountains all around this valley we're going to. It's going to be a lot hillier that the last ride we did. So what time do we have to leave? We want to arrive at the campsite by seven p.m.'

'I think we should catch the seven-fourteen train from Matfield,' said Toby finally.

Jay groaned. 'It's the half-term,' he said. 'We'll have to get up earlier than we do when we go to school.'

Toby gave him a shove. 'Don't be stupid,' he said. 'It's fun getting up early when you're going on holiday. And the later train doesn't get us there until two o'clock. If we go earlier, it makes the adventure last longer.'

Priya sat quietly and let the others make plans.

After a while she saw Rick crossing the field towards them.

'Well?' he said. 'Can I take a look?'

Toby had noted everything down in his jotter in his very neat handwriting.

'It all looks good,' Rick said. 'I'll take the number of this campsite. It sounds like the right kind of place – very simple facilities and they only take tents. It would be good if you could have a fire. I'll ask them. And you know the expedition has to have an objective, don't you? You haven't put that down yet.'

'This valley is where my grandfather was born,' said Andy. 'I've never been there, but my dad says our family lived there for hundreds of years. In that farm there . . .' He pointed to a place on the map.

'Greystone Farm,' said Rick. 'And it's right beside the river. It looks like a great place.'

'We thought we could find out about life in the valley today,' Connor said. 'We can see how it's changed since Andy's ancestors lived there.'

'Great idea!' Rick said.

Priya saw from the look on Andy's face that it meant a lot to him. She remembered the last time she had been back to India, when she was five years old. The heat and the smell. The bustling village in the middle of a dusty plain. She thought she knew how Andy felt.

'So, it's all settled?' asked Connor. 'We can do it?'

'I'll go now and call the campsite,' Rick said. 'But it's all looking good. Well done, Tigers.'

'There's a lot to do,' said Jay. 'We're going to have to fit carrier frames on all our bikes, and we'll have to work out how to strap the luggage on.'

'My dad's going to lend me some panniers,' Connor said. 'And my grandpa's got some too that he says we can borrow. Let's go and look at the tents.'

They went off to the store, chatting excitedly about the trip.

'We'll be taking these lightweight ones,'

Connor said, pulling an orange bag down from a high shelf and showing them to Jay and Priya. They hadn't been camping with the others before.

Jay took the tent from Connor and weighed it in his hands. 'It's still quite a lot to carry,' he said. 'Couldn't we split it up? One person could take the poles and the pegs and the other one could take the rest.'

'Good idea. I can share with Andy, and you can share with Toby, OK?'

The boys nodded. 'That leaves you and Abby,' Connor said to Priya. 'It's perfect.'

Priya tried to look pleased as Jay handed her the orange bundle, but she knew she was making a bad job of it. Luckily, Rick appeared in the doorway at just the right moment.

'I've spoken to the campsite owner,' he told them. 'He's a farmer in the next valley. He says there's no one else booked in for that night yet, so he'll keep it free for you and he's happy for you to have a campfire. He's even going to leave you some wood. And he also does bed and break-fast, Chris,' Rick continued, turning to Connor's dad, 'so you'll be able to keep an eye on this lot from a distance. As soon as I have the consent forms from your parents, you can go ahead and buy your tickets.'

At Scouts the following week, Abby was waiting on the grass with a tent bag in her hands. 'Listen,' she said to Priya, 'we have to get good at this. We don't often get the chance to prove to the boys that we're better than they are.'

'But I've never put one up before,' replied Priya.

'I have,' said Abby, shaking the tent out of its sack. A bag of poles and a smaller one of pegs fell out on top of the tent. 'You take the poles and put them together. I'll sort the tent out. Go on,' she said impatiently when Priya hesitated. 'They're all held together by elastic. It's easy, you'll see.'

Priya bit her lip and extracted the poles from

the bag. She picked one up and found that it was attached to a whole load of others. She moved it, and the short lengths of pole began to snap together. 'Hey!' she exclaimed. 'That's cool!'

'Told you.' Abby had laid the tent out on the ground. 'Now push that one through here, see?'

Priya inserted one end of the long, springy pole into the sleeve on the outside of the tent.

'That's it,' Abby said. 'Now fasten the end into that hole and hold the pole firm while I . . .' she grunted and the pole suddenly curved like a bow. 'Got it! Now the other one – quick!'

Priya took the other pole and quickly snapped it together, but in her rush she failed to notice that one of the sections hadn't gone in properly. She began shoving the pole into the sleeve, but suddenly it snagged in the fabric. 'Oh!' she said. 'I see what's happened. Hold on, I'll pull it out.'

'No!' yelled Abby. 'Stop!'

But she was too late. Priya had grabbed the end of the pole and yanked it, but all that happened was that the final section of pole came out and the elastic stretched and then snapped back, trapping the fabric of the tent.

'I'm really sorry,' said Priya. 'It's all a bit new to me.'

'Don't worry,' said Abby. 'I was much worse at the Summer Camp. I actually put a pole through the tent. Rick was really mad at me. When the pole gets stuck, you have to push, not pull. Then it all stays together. Here, we'll have to fit it back together through the sleeve, see?'

Abby bent over and began fiddling with the pole. Priya looked across and saw that the others had finished putting up their tents and were getting inside.

'Done it,' said Abby, bending the pole into shape. 'Now we just have to put the fly sheet on and we're done. It's dead simple. Go round the other side and peg it down.'

Priya did her best with the pegs, but Abby had to show her how to adjust their position so that there were no wrinkles in the fly sheet. By the time they'd finished the boys had gathered round to watch them.

'Good job,' said Connor.

'Bit slow, though,' observed Andy.

Abby chucked the tent bag at his head. 'Come on, Priya,' she said. 'Let's get inside, away from this lot.'

She unzipped the door and crawled in. Priya followed her. The orange light shining through the tent fabric seemed to glow.

Abby threw herself onto her back and looked up at the roof. 'Isn't it great?' she said. 'There's plenty of room. Lie down and you'll see.'

Priya stretched out beside her. She could hear the rattle of tent poles and the cries and laughter of the other Scouts and the scuffling of feet outside. It wasn't too bad. Maybe if she just closed her eyes for a moment and imagined it was dark . . .

Something scrabbled loudly against the wall of the tent. Priya screamed, and Abby started to laugh. 'It was Andy,' she said. 'He's always doing stuff like that. He thinks it's funny.' She stopped. 'Priya . . . ?' she whispered. 'What's the matter?'

'I'll never be able to do it,' Priya said. 'I won't ever be able to sleep in here in the dark. I can't help it, Abby. Please don't tell the others, though – say you won't!'

CHAPTER 7

It was the night before the expedition, and Priya was in a panic. Abby had been great. She had said nothing to the other Tigers, and she hadn't made a fuss.

'That's OK,' she'd said. 'We'll keep a torch on all night. I'll bring plenty of spare batteries. And you can get little night-lights for camping. We'll have one of those too. You're not the only one who's been scared of the dark, you know. Listen . . .'

Abby had been talking very quietly, but then she'd lowered her voice even further. 'You know Leanne in the Panthers? Last summer Julie had to call her dad to come and fetch her. He came all the way to Wales in the middle of the night.'

Abby had been great, but Priya knew that she

hadn't *really* understood. It wasn't the darkness *inside* the tent that bothered her. It was all the darkness *outside*. She was worried that she'd get to Wales and have to do just what Leanne had done. They'd have to do the worst thing of all – ask Connor's dad to help them – and the whole expedition would be wrecked. No. She couldn't let that happen.

Now, she took a deep breath and looked at her face in the mirror. 'I don't want to be scared,' she told her reflection. 'I don't *like* being scared. I don't look like a scared sort of person, do I?'

She smiled, and the serious brown face in the mirror smiled back at her. *I'm not even going to think about it*, she told herself. *I won't be on my own. I'll be with Abby, and we'll have torches, and I won't think about it again until we're actually there.*

She turned to the clothes that were neatly laid out on her bed and began to pack them in her pannier.

Connor was awake at dawn the next morning.

He threw open the window – it looked like it was going to be a perfect day. He went through the quiet house into the garden and checked his bike over carefully. When he came back inside, his dad was sitting at the kitchen table with a cup of coffee. 'You're up very early,' he said with a smile.

'I couldn't sleep,' Connor replied. 'I wanted to make sure everything was ready.' He picked up a small folder from the table and checked the train tickets inside. There were dozens of them – reservations for all their bikes, seat reservations, tickets . . .

'You checked all that last night,' laughed his dad. 'Why don't I make us some breakfast? I'll have to leave very soon after you lot.'

'Dad,' said Connor, 'you won't be watching us all the time, will you?'

His dad shook his head. 'I know it's annoying,' he said. 'When I did my first overnight expedition, we hiked over High Street in the Lakes and camped out in the hills. There were no grown-ups in sight – but then, our PL was nearly sixteen, and I suppose that made a difference.'

'You don't think I'm too young, do you?' asked Connor, suddenly anxious.

'Not at all,' replied Dr Sutcliff, putting a hand on his shoulder. 'I promise you, you won't even know I'm around unless something goes drastically wrong. I trust you, Connor, and Rick and Julie do too. We wouldn't be letting you do this if we didn't think you'd make a good job of it. Now, how many eggs would you like?'

At six o'clock, Connor was ready to leave. He wheeled his bike to the front gate and let his mum, who was still in her dressing gown, kiss him goodbye.

'Have a great time, love,' she said. 'And don't get into any scrapes.'

An upstairs window opened and Ellie leaned out. 'Stay away longer if you like. It'll be nice and quiet without you.'

Connor made a face. He couldn't stop himself.

'Off you go then,' said his dad. 'I'll see you at the station . . .'

'But . . .'

'I said I'll see you. You won't see me though. Then I'll check that you've arrived safely at the station in Wales, and later on at the campsite. Just make sure you remember to go to the checkpoint when you get to Birmingham. Once you're safely at the campsite, I'll be leaving you to it until the morning. That's not too bad, is it?'

'Thanks, Dad,' Connor said. He put on his helmet, jumped on his bike and rode off down the road. He had arranged to go to Priya's house and cycle to Andy's and Abby's with her. He couldn't help worrying a little about her. She was quite a bit younger than the rest of them, and even though he knew his dad was going to be around, he felt very responsible for her.

She was waiting outside the gate when he arrived, with her mum and dad and Mihir.

'Enjoy yourselves,' Mr Gupta called after them

as they prepared to set off. 'You're sure I can't come with you?'

Twenty minutes later the six Tigers arrived at the station. They were all talking excitedly as they wheeled their bikes through the entrance.

'We're half an hour early,' said Andy. 'I don't think I've ever been half an hour early in my life.'

'You wouldn't have been ready if I hadn't woken you up,' said Abby, who lived next door to him.

'I know.' Andy grinned. 'I don't think Dad was too pleased when you started knocking on the door at six o'clock though.'

'He would have had to get up anyway to go to work,' said Abby. 'I can't believe you slept through the alarm.'

'Well, we've made it,' said Jay. 'This is where the adventure begins—'

'Except it doesn't,' Toby interrupted. 'Look up there.'

They all looked at the information display

above their heads. Connor couldn't believe his eyes. The seven-fourteen train was cancelled! 'When's the next one?' he asked Toby. 'Have you got the timetable?'

Toby was already rummaging in his saddlebag. 'It's here,' he said, opening the booklet. 'There's one in an hour, but we'll never make the connection at Birmingham. Hold on though . . . Wait here.'

'What are you doing?' Jay called after him, but Toby didn't reply. He went into the ticket office and returned moments later clutching a sheaf of timetables. 'I thought so . . .' he said, scanning them rapidly. 'We can catch the seven-twenty to Helmetton from Platform Three and change there for a train to Birmingham. We'll have plenty of time to pick up the train to Wales.'

'But what about our tickets?' Connor asked. Toby seemed to think this was all very simple, but he wasn't so sure.

'Let me see them,' said Toby. 'I thought so. Look, it says: *All routes. Not London*. We won't be going through London, so it's fine.'

Connor breathed a sigh of relief. 'Come on, then,' he said. 'Let's go to Platform Three.'

They pushed their bikes towards the waiting train and stopped beside a door with a picture of a bike stencilled on it. Connor pushed the button and the door hissed open to reveal a uniformed guard. 'Have you got reservations for those?' he demanded, looking suspiciously at the bikes.

'Yes,' Connor replied. 'At least, they were reserved on the seven-fourteen to Baxford Junction, but it's been cancelled.'

'That's a different train,' said the guard. 'I can't take those bikes, I'm afraid.'

'Excuse me, sir,' said Jay politely, stepping forward. 'I thought it said in your leaflet that you always carry bikes if there's room?'

The guard bristled. 'Bicycles are carried at the discretion of the guard, young man. You'll just have to go away and make new reservations, I'm afraid. There's nothing I can do. It's the rules, see?'

Connor's heart sank. By the time they'd made

new reservations the train would have left. They'd be late at the Birmingham checkpoint and they'd miss their connection at Birmingham and there was no way they'd get to Wales in time. He thought of his dad waiting at the station, checking that they had arrived. He was going to have to call him, right at the beginning of the expedition, before they'd even done anything. He reached for his phone. Then he looked up and saw Jay leap on his bike and cycle rapidly away down the platform.

'Oi!' the guard called after him. 'That's not allowed, that isn't. Get off that bike!'

'What's he doing now?' Connor asked Toby, frowning.

Jay had caused trouble before by running off in a temper. Connor stared after him, and to his astonishment saw him skid to a halt beside a tall man in a uniform. He was talking animatedly, pointing back towards the train. After a few moments the uniformed man began walking towards them, with Jay beside him, pushing his bike. The guard waited with a surly expression on his face.

'Good morning, everyone,' said the tall man when he reached them. 'I'm the supervisor here. Your friend tells me you had reservations on the seven-fourteen. Can I see them, please?'

Connor fumbled for the tickets and gave them to him.

'OK,' he said. 'Let's see what we can do.'

'They can't put them in here,' said the guard. 'What about the rules?'

'They've paid their money,' said the supervisor. 'So why don't we make sure they get what they've paid for . . .' He hopped onto the train and looked inside. 'There's bags of room,' he told the guard. 'Come on, you lot. Let's get them in. We don't want this train delayed, do we, Barry?'

The guard stood back and watched glumly as they loaded up their bikes.

'Thanks very much,' Connor said to the supervisor when they were all securely in place.

'You should thank your friend,' said the

supervisor. 'Quick thinking, that was. No less than I'd expect from a Scout, of course. I was one myself, a long time ago. Just make sure you don't ride your bike along the platform again, OK? Have a good trip!'

The Tigers made their way to their seats. 'Phew!' said Connor as the train pulled out of the station. 'That was really close. Brilliant, Jay! I would never have had the nerve.'

'I didn't know if it would work,' said Jay, 'but I saw the supervisor – and we did have res-ervations, after all.'

'Well, now we can stop worrying,' Abby said. 'We're properly on our way at last.'

CHAPTER 8

The Tigers had no trouble on the rest of their journey. By arrangement with Rick, a local Scout Leader was waiting to check them in at the busy station in Birmingham. They found their way to their next train, and an hour later they were cycling slowly through a small Welsh town. There was only one main street, but that was buzzing with cars and people, and there was a small market in the square at the top.

'I've got to film this,' Andy said, so they all leaned their bikes against a wall and waited in the sunshine while he took some shots of the bustling market square.

'You lot just carry on,' he said to the waiting Tigers. 'I can always catch you up.'

'Yeah, right,' laughed Abby. 'You'd get lost and we'd never see you again.'

'We all stay together,' said Connor firmly. 'Even if we don't arrive at the campsite until the middle of the night!'

'Hey!' protested Andy. 'My movie's important. You all know that. I'm making a film about my journey back to the land of my ancestors.' He stopped, and the other Tigers all burst out laughing.

'Of course you have to make your film,' said Connor. 'That's why we came. It's just – you're so easy to wind up. Can we go now?'

Priya gazed around as they moved off through the marketplace. It was the first time she'd been in a new place without the rest of her family, and she loved listening to the unfamiliar Welsh lilt in the voices of the passers-by. It had been a bad moment when the train had been cancelled, and an even worse one when the guard had refused to let their bikes on, but Jay had been amazing. She looked at her friends. *I won't let them down*, she told herself. *I'm going to enjoy it.*

Toby checked the map and they headed off down a side street and through a small council estate. They rode along an alleyway, and for a moment Priya thought they must have gone wrong, but they suddenly emerged beside a busy main road.

'We haven't got to cycle along here, have we?' she asked Connor. 'It looks dangerous.'

'Don't worry,' he said. 'There's a cycleway.'

'But it's on the other side of the road,' Abby pointed out.

They all stared. A car flashed by at speed, a blur of red.

'I'm sorry,' Toby said. 'I thought I'd found a clever short cut, but we can't cross the road here. We'll have to go all the way back into town.'

'That's daft,' said Jay. 'It's not that busy. We can just wait for a gap in the traffic.'

'No way,' said Connor.

'Jay's right,' said Andy. 'There's nothing coming. Let's go.'

Andy and Jay didn't wait for Connor to reply, but set off at once across the road.

'Idiots!' shouted Connor, but the two boys were already on the far side of the road, laughing.

'It's easy,' Jay called back. 'Hurry!'

Connor hesitated. There was no traffic in sight. 'Go on then,' he said to Abby, Priya and Toby. 'It'll save time.'

Priya crossed quickly with the others beside her. She was in the middle of the road when she heard the roar of approaching cars. She hurried to the far side. As she reached it, Connor rushed past her, pushing his bike onto the grassy verge. At the same moment a truck growled past, buffeting them in the dusty wind of its slipstream. They all stood looking at each other.

Jay spoke first, red-faced. 'I'm sorry,' he said. 'That was really stupid.'

'Right,' agreed Andy. 'Sorry, everyone.'

'It's my fault,' said Toby. 'I should have looked at the map more carefully.'

'You know what?' Abby realized. 'Roads are

just as dangerous as cliff faces and snowstorms and frozen ponds. We have to be careful. You're an idiot, Andy – and you too, Jay.'

'And I should have stopped them,' said Connor, and Priya could see that he was shaken. 'Luckily that's the only big road we have to cross. We have to cycle along here for about five kilometres and then we turn off. Let's get on with it.'

It wasn't much fun, following the cycleway beside the road while an endless succession of trucks and buses and cars raced past them. Priya kept looking away to her left, where a line of blue hills rose in the hazy distance. At last they reached a junction where a tiny side road led off towards the west, and the Scouts turned down it.

Priya felt as if she was suddenly in a different world. She could hear the birds singing in the green hedgerows and lambs bleating in the fields. The roar of the main road quickly faded, and the sun was warm on her face. A skylark began to sing somewhere overhead. After a hundred metres, another lane branched off and there was a triangle of grass in the middle of the junction.

'Let's stop here for a bit,' said Connor, laying his bike down on the grass.

'It feels like we've been travelling for ever.' Abby looked at her watch. 'But it's only half past eleven.'

'We've hardly started,' said Toby. 'We've got thirty kilometres to go, but it should be simple from here.' He spread the map out on the grass and they all gathered round to look.

Priya munched on a chocolate bar as Toby pointed out their route. It zigzagged at first through gentle hills, but about halfway the contour lines were drawn so close together on either side of the road that the map looked brown. 'It looks steep,' she said.

'I know,' replied Toby. 'But it's not quite as bad as it looks because we follow the river. We don't actually have to cycle over any mountains.'

'I'd rather cycle over mountains than go through all that traffic,' said Priya.

The others nodded, and she knew they

were all remembering crossing the busy road.

'Let's not make any more mistakes,' said Connor. 'We'll ride carefully, and if we hear a car coming we'll stop. These lanes are really narrow.'

They cycled on for eight uneventful kilometres and saw only one car – a battered green Land Rover covered in mud. It didn't slow down at all as it passed them and Connor was glad that they had pulled carefully to one side. Later they were forced to wait as a herd of cows wandered across the road and through a gate, followed by a farmer and a small wiry dog. The farmer grinned at them and raised a hand as they picked their way through the green cow-pats that were splattered across the road. Shortly afterwards they coasted down a long hill and arrived at a stone bridge over a small river.

'This is it,' said Andy excitedly. 'This is the Afon Ddu. The Black River. It starts way up in the hills beyond my grandpa's farm. I have to film this. Why don't I get a shot of all of you coming down the hill. Go back up and do it again.'

They all groaned. 'Come on,' said Abby. 'We should do what he says. You know it'll be worth it.'

So they all went a short way back up the hill and freewheeled down towards the waiting Andy. He showed them the clip on the screen of his camera. 'See?' he said. 'You look like a team.'

Priya saw herself racing down the hill, her face split by a grin, her scarf fluttering and her hair streaming out behind her. Then the camera panned round to the river and up towards the cleft in the hills where they were heading. The clip finished, and she looked up at the real hills as the sun went behind a cloud. 'It looks wild up there,' she said.

'Don't worry,' Abby reassured her as the others cycled off ahead of them. 'We're going to be really cosy in our tent. You'll see.'

'I know,' said Priya. 'Thanks, Abby. I'm fine.'

But inside, she wasn't quite so sure.

As they cycled along beside the river, Connor

replayed the morning's events in his head. There was nothing he could have done about the cancelled train, although it would have been sensible to have a backup plan. Still, thanks to Jay it had worked out OK. But he should have stopped Jay crossing that road, and he should never have followed him. The road had been empty one moment, and full of speeding traffic the next. It had happened so fast. He shuddered, thinking of it. He should have paid more attention when Toby had been planning the route. It had been obvious on the map where they should have gone. His dad had trusted him to look after everyone, and so far he was doing a bad job. The others all seemed to be having a great time, but Connor couldn't help feeling that they weren't taking it seriously enough.

'Connor, look!' called Abby, interrupting his gloomy thoughts. 'On the other side of the river.'

They all stopped and looked where she was pointing. In a field on the opposite hillside a flock of sheep was on the move. As Connor watched, he saw that three black-and-white dogs were herding the sheep, moving and stopping, advancing and retreating, as a man by the gate called out commands in a sharp, high-pitched voice.

Andy immediately got out his camcorder and began shooting. 'This is where the zoom really comes in handy,' he said. 'But it's hard to keep it steady. Here, Abby. Keep shooting.'

Andy handed the camcorder to her and pulled a tiny flexible tripod out of his bag. Somehow he set the tripod and the camera on top of the stone wall. For once, no one was impatient with Andy's movie-making. Connor couldn't keep his eyes off the dogs. They worked together, a perfect team, and the sheep funnelled obediently down through a gate and into a pen. The farmer closed the gate, then jumped onto a quad bike. The three dogs leaped into the trailer behind him and he drove off down the hillside.

'That's amazing!' Andy's eyes were shining. 'I got every single bit of it! Why do you think he's put the sheep in the pen?'

'I don't know,' said Toby. 'But we can't wait to find out. We've still got a long way to go.'

'Yeah, OK,' said Andy. 'But it was worth stopping, wasn't it?' He paused. 'Hey, do you think sheep-farming's in my blood?'

They all laughed. 'You're not going to want to go home tomorrow, are you?' Abby said to him.

They started out once more, Jay leading the way. 'You look worried,' Toby said, slowing down to ride beside Connor. 'But we're doing OK, you know. There are always going to be hiccups on a trip like this.'

'I know what Jay's like,' Connor said. 'He does things before he thinks. I should have been ready.'

'It's not all down to you,' Toby replied. 'I'm the APL, remember? And this is great, isn't it? We're on our own and we're exploring.'

'I suppose. But we are responsible for that lot, remember.'

'And they're doing fine. We'd better catch them up.'

The narrow road climbed more steeply now, and the hills drew more closely together ahead of them, squeezing the river into a narrow gorge overhung with trees. The sound of rushing water was loud in the valley, but then, quite suddenly, they reached the top of the climb and the road levelled out. The hills were set further back and there were green fields beside the river.

'It's like a secret valley,' said Abby. 'I want to go ahead. I'll be the first one to explore it.'

'People *have* been here before, you know,' laughed Andy, letting her overtake him, pedalling hard. 'My grandparents, for instance.'

'Hey, Abby, wait!' called Toby, but she didn't stop.

'She's OK,' said Andy. 'You can see the road all the way up the valley. And not a car in sight.'

'OK, then,' Connor said to the others, with a glance at Toby. 'We'll have to go faster too. Why is it so hard to get everyone to stay together?'

'We do when it matters,' said Jay. Then he

stopped. 'Yeah, OK,' he agreed. 'Let's catch her up.'

They all raced after Abby. Connor watched for a second, then set off in pursuit. The road was deceptive. It had looked flat after the long climb from the bridge, but they were still pedalling uphill and it was hard work. Connor was soon sweating as he sprinted to catch up with the others, pushing himself as hard as he could. There was a sudden roar, and he felt something big rush past him, so close that he wasn't sure afterwards if it had touched him or not. Then he was struggling to control his bike. His front wheel went off the road and he felt himself slipping sideways down a stony bank. The bike crashed down on top of him and something tore at his face. Then he was lying on his back with his face on fire, looking up at the sky as a bicycle wheel spun round and round at the edge of his vision. He heard the voices of the others calling urgently from up above.

CHAPTER 9

Toby was the first to arrive, slithering down the stony slope towards him. 'Are you OK?' he asked anxiously.

'Your head!' cried Abby. 'What have you done?'

'What happened?' said Toby. 'I'm going to call your dad.'

'No!' said Connor urgently. He was still lying on his back. His leg hurt, but his face hurt worse. He put his hand up to his cheek and it came away covered in blood. 'It was that car. I think it might have hit me. Then I just sort of fell.' A thought struck him. 'My bike!' he said. 'Is it OK?'

'Hold on . . .' Jay grabbed the bike and lifted it off him. 'It looks all right,' he said. 'I think you might have broken its fall!'

Connor laughed, in spite of the pain. Priya was kneeling beside him with a tissue in her hand. 'Let me wipe some of that blood away,' she said.

'Wait,' said Toby. 'Connor, did you black out? Which bits of you hurt?'

'I remember everything,' Connor told him. 'My leg hurts a bit, but my face is worse. It feels like it's on fire.'

'OK,' Toby said to Priya.

Connor waited anxiously as she unclipped his helmet and cleaned his face.

'That's amazing!' she said. 'All that blood from a tiny little cut!'

Connor felt almost disappointed.

'Hang on,' she went on. 'It's not all blood. Your face is very red underneath.'

'It really stings,' he told her.

'I'm not surprised,' called Andy from further up the slope. 'You fell right through the middle of all these nettles. And there are thorns here too.'

Connor sat up and looked into the anxious

eyes of the other Tigers. 'I think I'm all right,' he said. 'I'm going to stand up.'

Toby held out a hand and Connor grabbed it and pulled himself upright. He winced with pain as he put his weight on his right leg, and lurched against Toby. He tried again, and this time the leg held him. 'Help me up there,' he said, looking up at the road. 'I think it's all right.'

With Jay and Toby on either side of him, Connor struggled to the top. When they reached the road, he walked slowly up and down. 'It's like when you get kicked playing football,' he said as the others watched him anxiously. 'I expect it'll stop hurting after a while.'

He looked down at his legs. They were grazed by the fall and scratched by brambles. He pulled up the leg of his shorts and felt his thigh gingerly. He knew he'd been very lucky, and just for a moment he felt dizzy. Then the world righted itself again and he saw Jay wheeling his bike along the road. It was making a horrible scraping sound.

'Don't worry,' Jay said. 'It's only the mudguard. I can fix it.'

'You should sit down for a bit,' Toby said seriously. 'Have a drink and something to eat, and then we can decide what to do.'

'What do you mean?'

'Well, you should probably see a doctor,' Toby told him. 'Just to make sure.'

'I told you,' Connor insisted. 'I'm completely fine.'

But then his legs suddenly turned to jelly and he found himself sitting on the grass. Toby opened one of his panniers and took out a small stove. 'I'm going to make Connor a cup of tea,' he said. 'Anyone else want one?'

The others all shook their heads.

'I don't need tea,' Connor said. 'A drink from my bottle will be fine.'

But Toby insisted on filling a pan, boiling water, and making Connor a cup of tea. 'Biscuit?' he said, offering Connor a ginger nut before handing the packet round.

Connor laughed. The throbbing in his leg was easier now, although his face was stinging worse than ever. He was starting to feel better. Toby had been clever, making him wait for the water to boil; forcing him to sit still instead of getting on his bike. He sipped the sweet steaming tea gratefully and looked around. Jay was doing something to his bike and Andy was busy with his camera. 'Where are Abby and Priya?' he asked.

'Here,' said Abby. She was climbing up from the riverbank with a bunch of leaves in her hand. 'Docks,' she told him. 'You can rub them on your stings.'

'Thanks,' said Connor, pressing the cool green leaves against his cheeks. 'That feels good. It's not a good idea, stinging your face.'

'Neither is falling off your bike,' said Abby. 'We all got off the road. How come you didn't?'

'I wasn't paying attention,' Connor admitted, embarrassed. 'I was trying to catch you up. None of you got hurt, did you?'

'We were all off the road,' Abby said. 'Toby heard the car coming and warned us.'

'OK.' Connor handed his cup to Toby. 'I'm ready now. We'd better carry on. We've lost a lot of time.'

'Wait,' said Toby. 'I don't mind going on, but if you feel sick or dizzy you have to tell us straight away, OK? I know you don't think you blacked out, but you rolled a long way down there. And keep an eye on that bruise.'

Connor looked down and saw a big, dark red mark on his leg.

'It's going to be a good one,' Toby told him. 'Just take it easy at first, OK?'

Connor nodded. Jay wheeled his bike over to him. 'I've straightened out the mudguard,' he said. 'Everything else is OK.'

'Thanks,' said Connor, watching Toby as he spoke to the others. Toby seemed to have taken charge. He couldn't hear what he was saying, but he guessed he was telling them to go slowly. He still felt a little shaky, and when he got on his bike he couldn't stop himself grimacing at the pain in his leg as he turned the pedals.

'Jay's going in front,' Toby said. 'I'll go at the back. We're all going to ride in a low gear.'

They pedalled on up the valley. The road climbed gradually as the river tumbled in a rocky bed below them. The valley was still wide, with small fields on either side of it, the green hillsides crisscrossed by a haphazard mixture of walls and hedges. They passed occasional farms, low grey buildings with barns and sheds attached to them. Connor was relieved to find that his leg was feeling better. The throbbing pain had turned to a dull ache and he had no trouble keeping up with the others.

Sheep were everywhere. A few kilometres further on they saw a cattle grid in the road ahead of them.

'We'll have to watch out,' said Abby. 'Look – they're just lying in the road.'

Sure enough, on the far side of the cattle grid several yellow-eyed sheep were watching them.

As they pushed their bikes over the slats, the sheep scrambled to their feet and ran off towards the river across tussocky slopes.

'I don't think they like us,' laughed Andy. 'They could be quite scary if you met them on a dark night.'

On their right there were no fields now, just grassy hillside dotted with sheep. A short distance further on they passed a gateway on their left when Jay gave a shout and stopped his bike. 'Look down there!'

A rough track led down towards the river between stone walls. At the foot of the track, a dirty green Land Rover was parked. 'It's the one that knocked you over,' Jay said. 'I'm sure it is.'

'You can't know that,' said Connor. 'There's been one in almost every farm we've passed.'

'Actually, Jay's right . . .' Toby had been leafing through his notebook. 'I wrote the registration number down.'

'Toby!' said Priya. 'Do you write down the number of every car we see?'

'I remembered it. And when I realized it had caused an accident, I thought I should make a note of it,' he explained when he saw the way the others were looking at him.

'So what if it is the same one?' asked Andy after a moment. 'What do you want to do? Go and tell them off?'

'Andy's right,' said Connor. 'And anyway, there's no one there. I don't especially want to meet them. Let's get going.'

They continued along the road, crested a low rise, and saw the valley open out ahead of them. The broad valley bottom was divided into fields, and the hills were higher, but further away, hazy in the afternoon sunshine.

'We must be nearly there,' said Andy, pulling an old black-and-white photograph out of his pocket. 'Look, this is my grandpa. It's the same place!'

They all gathered round to look at the picture. A small grinning boy was facing the camera. Beside him was a man with a face burned dark by the sun, and a couple of dogs just like the ones they'd seen earlier. They were standing on a road, and behind them Connor could see the distinctive outline of the hills.

'You can see the river,' Andy told the others. 'And the bridge. Look – there it is!'

He pointed, and Connor saw that the road descended gently ahead of them and crossed the river over a low bridge.

'I wouldn't say "nearly there" exactly,' commented Toby, looking at the map. 'We've got nearly ten kilometres to go. We—'

He was interrupted by a cry from Priya. 'Over here!' she said. 'It's a sheep. I think it's hurt.'

'Oh, the poor thing!' gasped Abby. 'Look, it's hurt its leg!'

The sheep was lying very still. Its left front leg was bloody.

'We'll have to tell someone,' Connor said. 'Toby, where's the nearest farm?'

'Over the bridge,' he replied. 'It's not far. You could see it if that hill wasn't in the way.'

'Right then. We'll go there.'

'I'll stay with the sheep,' Abby said. 'We can't leave it on its own.'

'We have to,' Connor insisted. 'Things go wrong when we split up. We won't be long.'

Abby reluctantly got on her bike, and they cycled down the hill and over the bridge. The river looped to the right, and they soon saw the farm buildings clustered together about half a mile from the road. They cycled up a stony track and stopped when four dogs confronted them, barking wildly.

'That'll do!' came a sharp cry from the farmhouse door. The dogs instantly turned and ran back to their master, a short, stocky man with a red face and very blue eyes. He had a fifth dog at his side. He looked them over and then said, 'You'll be lost, I dare say. You'll be wanting the campsite. It's four miles that way. There's no camping here.' He pointed up the valley with his stick. The dogs lay, watchful, at his feet.

'I'm sorry,' said Connor. 'We didn't mean to

trespass or anything. It's just that we found a sheep lying by the road. It's been injured. We thought we should tell someone.'

'It's probably asleep,' said the farmer. 'I get tourists coming up here all the time. They get lazy in the sunshine.'

'No,' said Abby urgently. 'I think it's been hit by a car. Its leg is all bloody.'

'Oh,' said the farmer gruffly. 'I see. Well then, that's different. Thank you for telling me. Where is it, exactly?'

'It's not far,' Connor told him. 'We can show you if you like.'

The farmer walked over to a quad bike and jumped onto it with surprising agility. 'Meg! Jenny!' he called, and two of the dogs streaked across the yard and jumped up beside him. He waved at the Tigers. 'Lead on – I'll follow you.'

They rattled back down the track with the quad bike chugging behind them. Then they sprinted back along the road, with Jay in the lead, and halted beside the injured sheep.

'By God, I'd like to get hold of the person who did this,' said the farmer as he gently examined the damaged leg. The sheep suddenly kicked out as his fingers moved, and he spoke soothingly. Then he looked up. 'She's had a lucky escape. Nothing broken, I don't think, but she's in shock. These tourists – they come driving along these roads at ridiculous speeds. They don't care about anyone but themselves. They don't even have the courtesy to come and tell us what they've done. They would have left this poor creature to suffer.'

'Connor got knocked off his bike earlier,' Abby told him. 'I don't think it was a tourist though. They were in a dirty old Land Rover. It's parked back down the road.'

'Maybe it was the same people,' said Andy. 'They didn't stop for Connor either.'

'Where did you say it was parked?' demanded the farmer.

Toby already had the map in his hand. He pointed out the place.

'That's my land,' the man said angrily. 'Even if it wasn't them who did this, they've no right to be parking down there. Wait here – I'm going to give them a piece of my mind.'

'I shouldn't have said anything,' Abby said as the quad bike roared off down the road. 'What if there's a fight?'

'There's nothing we can do now,' said Connor. 'We'll just have to wait.'

CHAPTER 10

Priya knelt by the injured sheep and gently placed her hand on the ragged, dirty fleece. A strong smell came off the matted wool. She supposed it must be the smell of sheep. 'You're going to be fine,' she murmured, stroking the sheep's back as the sound of the farmer's quad bike faded. She had been horrified when she'd seen the bloody leg, but now it seemed that, like Connor's, the injury wasn't as bad as they'd all imagined.

She looked up. The others were all gazing after the farmer.

'He was very angry,' said Andy.

'Wouldn't you be?' Jay asked. 'I don't think he likes visitors much. Maybe we should just get going.'

'No,' said Connor at once. 'He asked us to stay here with the sheep. How's she doing, Priya?'

'All right, I think,' Priya said. 'You know what, though? She's quite skinny under all this wool. It's amazingly thick.'

One by one, the other Tigers knelt beside the sheep and felt the thickness of her fleece and the thinness of the body beneath it.

'Here comes the farmer again.' Andy had his camera out and now swivelled round to film the quad bike racing back up the road.

They all stood up, but Priya remained beside the sheep.

'Gone,' said the farmer shortly, jumping off the bike. 'But I'd like to know what they were up to down there. You say you never saw who was inside?'

They all shook their heads. 'Just the Land Rover,' Connor said. 'But Toby wrote down its number.'

The farmer looked at Toby and nodded approval. 'Good lad,' he said. 'I'll take that off you before you go. Chances are they were just trippers out for a walk. There's no footpath down there, but that never seems to stop people. Now then, one of you'd better give me a hand to get this beast up onto the bike. My back's not as strong as it used to be.'

'I'll do it,' said Abby at once.

'Can I help too?' asked Priya.

'Why not?' he replied, smiling suddenly. 'You seem to have made friends with her. Everyone ready? I'll count to three. One . . . two . . . three . . . lift!'

They laid the sheep on the platform at the front of the bike. The farmer put a strap across her, then looked round at the Tigers. 'Well now,' he said. 'You've done me a real favour, and you look to me as if you might be in need of a little refreshment. You must have cycled a long way. Come and have a bite to eat with me and the wife. My name's Jones, by the way. Thomas Jones.'

'Thank you very much, Mr Jones,' said

Connor, glancing around at the others. 'We'd love to!' He introduced himself and the other members of Tiger Patrol.

Back at the farm, Mr Jones opened the door of a small stone shed. 'She can stay in here,' he said, sending Andy and Toby to fetch a bale of straw from the other side of the yard. He shook out the straw on the floor of the shed, and then Priya and Abby carefully helped him to lay the sheep down.

'Whatever is all this fuss, Thomas?' came a voice from the house. Priya saw a small woman with short grey hair and a brown face coming across the yard towards them. Mr Jones quickly explained, and his wife immediately ran back to the house and returned with a medical kit and a bucket of water. The Tigers watched as she cleaned the sheep's injured leg with nimble fingers and then applied a bandage. As soon as she'd finished, the sheep scrabbled to her feet. 'Not a lot wrong with her,' Mrs Jones said. 'She's a lucky girl.'

'We'll keep her inside for the night,' said her husband. 'Just to be on the safe side.'

'And what about you?' Mrs Jones was staring at Connor. 'You look as if you've been in the wars. Let me see to that cut.'

Priya saw that the cut on his eyebrow was trickling blood again, and his legs were covered in small scratches. His clothes were a mess.

'Come on inside,' Mrs Jones said. 'I'll fix up this young man and then we'll all have a cup of tea and you can tell us about your adventures.'

They followed her into the farmhouse through the low front door; then she led Connor and Toby into the kitchen while Mr Jones told the others to take a seat in a low-ceilinged room with a loud ticking clock. They sat around an ancient table that shone darkly with years of polishing.

'I thought Connor looked a bit sheepish,' Abby said, and they all laughed.

'Even his hair was matted,' said Andy. 'I got it all on my camera. There were bits of twigs in it.'

'You're lucky it ended so well,' said Mr Jones,

returning from the kitchen. 'Two nasty accidents and nobody badly hurt. That deserves a small celebration, I think.'

Connor and Toby reappeared, Connor looking a lot cleaner, and shortly afterwards Mrs Jones came in carrying a massive teapot and some mugs on a silver tray. Her husband poured out the tea and then she brought in a plate loaded with sandwiches, and an apple pie. 'Get stuck in,' she said. 'You've earned it!'

Half an hour later most of the sandwiches had been eaten, along with half the apple pie. 'I'm not sure I'm going to be able to cycle any further,' said Jay. 'In fact, I'm not sure I can move.'

'Of course you can,' said Toby. 'We've got another six kilometres to go. We have to get to the campsite or the expedition won't count.'

'You don't have to set off right away, do you?' said Mr Jones. 'I have to bring some sheep down from the top pasture and I thought you might like to see the dogs working.'

'That would be great,' Priya said. 'Wouldn't it, Connor?'

Mr and Mrs Jones had both been chatting non-stop while the Tigers had been eating. There were photos of their four grown-up children on the mantelpiece and on the windowsill, and the Tigers had heard all about them. Priya had the feeling that, although the farmer had been grumpy at first, he was pleased to have some company.

'We really ought to get on . . .' Connor began, but there was a chorus of disagreement from the others.

'We don't have to be at the campsite until seven,' Toby commented. 'We've got plenty of time. It's only three-thirty.'

'What about visiting Andy's great-grandfather's farm?' asked Connor. 'We have to do that too.'

'What's all this?' asked Mr Jones. 'Your great-grandfather, you say?'

'He lived at a place called Greystone Farm,' Andy said.

'You'll be going right past it,' the farmer replied. 'Your great-grandfather must have been Dafydd Williams. Wait a moment – I've got a photograph somewhere.'

He searched in a cupboard and pulled out an old photo album. 'There you are!' he said triumphantly, pointing to a faded brown photograph of two young, curly-haired men and a small boy. 'Your great-grandfather, and my dad and me!'

He took the photo out of the album and handed it to Andy, who for once could think of nothing to say.

'I'll scan it for you,' said Mrs Jones immediately. 'Then I can email it to you, can't I?'

'Thanks,' said Andy. 'That's amazing.'

'Oh, don't look so surprised,' she told him. 'I love my computer. That's how I keep in touch with my children.'

'You won't find a lot to see at Greystone though,' said Mr Jones. 'It's right on the road, by the bridge, but it's a weekend place now. The people who own it live in London. They only come about twice a year. I doubt there'll be anyone there.'

'Dafydd got out of farming at the right time,' Mrs Jones said. 'The children are always telling us we're daft to stay on. They want us to retire.'

'Well, I don't want to live in a bungalow in a town, Gladys,' her husband said hotly. 'This is my home and I don't want to see it turned into a holiday place. No I don't.'

'We might not have a choice,' Mrs Jones pointed out, 'if the price of feed keeps going up.'

'Or if there's more trouble with thieves,' added the farmer darkly. 'But come on, it's a lovely evening. I'll show you what these dogs can do.'

Out in the yard once more, Mr Jones called the dogs over. They sniffed suspiciously at the children and then ignored them completely. Priya ran across and looked over the half-door of the shed to check on the sheep. She was lying in the straw, her flanks rising and falling as she slept peacefully. Priya couldn't help yawning herself. The good food and the exercise had made her sleepy.

'Hurry up, Priya!' yelled Abby, and she turned and saw the others disappearing up a rough track. She ran to catch up with them and realized that Mr Jones had sent the three dogs on ahead, streaking over the drystone walls into the topmost field, where a flock of sheep were grazing.

'Why are you moving them?' asked Toby.

'You may well ask,' said Mr Jones grimly. 'I bring as many as I can down close to the house at night because there are people about who want to steal them.'

'Steal them?' exclaimed Connor. 'Do people really do that?'

'Oh, yes.'

Priya was horrified. 'You don't mean they kill them?' she asked.

'Bless you, no. They're clever, these thieves. They know how to move them. They use dogs, just like I do. They come in the night and they take them away in trucks. My neighbour in the next valley lost fifty sheep last month. You see, our farms are very big. Mine goes right over those hilltops there and all along the valley nearly as far as the bridge. So you see, I can't keep all the sheep safe at night.'

The farmer broke off and called out a couple of sharp commands to the dogs. The sheep had gathered together in the middle of the field and two of the dogs ran round behind them and began to push them with little movements towards the gate that Mr Jones was now holding open.

'Is that why you were so worried about that Land Rover?' Connor asked him suddenly as the sheep began to stream past them into the lower field.

'That's right. We all keep an eye out for strange vehicles. And we keep a note of their numbers too,' he added, with a nod to Toby. 'But there's a lot of land and a lot of sheep, and not many farmers. You can't be watching all the time.'

'They're like rustlers,' said Jay, 'in the Wild West.'

'They're nothing but common thieves,' Mr Jones said bitterly as he closed the gate and they walked back down the track. When they arrived at the yard once more, he thanked them again for helping with the sheep. 'You know, you could always camp in that field if you wanted to,' he said, pointing to a level green pasture beside the river. 'You could use the bathroom in the house, and I dare say we could fix you up with a nice fried breakfast in the morning.'

'That would be fantastic,' Priya said. 'We could keep an eye on the sheep and we wouldn't have to cycle any further—' She stopped.

Connor was shaking his head. 'I'm sorry, Mr Jones,' he said. 'We have to stick to our plan. Someone will be checking that we get to the campsite on time. And anyway, we have to visit Greystone Farm. It's our main objective. Maybe we can call in and see how that sheep is doing on our way home tomorrow?'

Priya tried to hide her disappointment. Sleeping in a field near a friendly farmhouse didn't seem anything like as daunting as camping out in the wild. She knew they were going to a campsite, but the hills ahead of them looked high and bleak, and Mr Jones had already told them that there was no one else living further up the valley. She fetched her bike, put on her helmet and joined the others as they cycled down the bumpy track. They paused at the bottom and looked back to see Mr and Mrs Jones waving them on their way.

'It would be awful if they had to leave,' Andy said.

'It looks so quiet,' added Abby. 'You'd never think all that stuff happened.'

'Well, we wanted to find out what it was like to live here,' Toby said. 'And no one can say we haven't done that.'

'But we've definitely had enough trouble for one trip,' Connor sighed. 'Or I have, anyway. Let's get to the campsite.'

'They were really nice,' said Priya as they cycled on. 'It's a shame we couldn't stay.'

'You wait,' Abby told her. 'You wait until we're camped and we get the fire going. You'll be glad then that we didn't.'

Priya wasn't so sure.

CHAPTER 11

'It's a shame we couldn't stop there,' Connor said to Priya as they rode away from the farm. 'It would have been fun, but my dad would get really worried if we didn't show up at the campsite!'

'I know,' said Priya. 'Hey, look! There are cows.'

They all stopped to peer over the hedge. There were two fields and a narrow strip of trees between the road and the river, and the cows were grazing the nearer field.

'It makes a change from sheep,' said Andy, whipping out his camera. 'Do you think these belong to Mr Jones?'

'He said that his land went all the way to the next bridge,' replied Toby. 'So they must do. There's a footpath through the field. I bet you can walk down to the river.'

'I don't think so,' said Abby, and they all looked at her in surprise.

'You said you weren't scared of them on the night hike,' Andy said. 'You said it was because you thought it was a bull.'

'OK, OK!' she said quickly. 'I don't really like cows, that's all. When I was little my mum held me up to see one and it licked my face.' She shuddered. 'It was horrible. Like warm, wet sandpaper.'

They were all laughing as they cycled on. To their left, the fields slanted up the hillside between stone walls. They could hear the river beyond the trees to their right, but most of the time it stayed hidden from view. Connor's leg was hurting again, but he didn't want the others to know that, so he gritted his teeth and kept pedalling.

The road climbed steadily upwards, and suddenly a view opened up all around. 'There it is!' Andy stopped his bike and pointed ahead. 'That's where my great-grandfather lived.

Imagine! If he hadn't left, then I might be living there now.'

'But then you wouldn't be living next door to me,' Abby told him. 'It looks kind of lonely, doesn't it?'

Connor stopped beside Andy as he took his camcorder out again. The farm buildings were still nearly a mile away, clustered together on the far side of a low bridge, but even from this distance they could see that it wasn't a working farm. There were no tractors or farm machinery in the yard; no sign of straw or hay in the buildings; and there were new-looking fences and gates.

'At least it's downhill all the way there,' Connor said.

'But not all the way to the campsite,' Toby replied with a smile. He had been scanning the opposite side of the valley with his binoculars and now he handed them to Connor. 'You can see it,' he said. 'See how the road goes up the other side? If you follow it along, there's a house and a couple of sheds and a blue sign. That's the campsite.'

Connor examined the steep climb and let out a sigh.

'What's up, Connor?' asked Abby. 'It's your leg, isn't it?'

'It does hurt a bit,' he admitted, wincing. 'But I'm sure it'll be OK after I have a rest. Come on, let's go down to the farm.'

They freewheeled gently downhill all the way to the bridge. The afternoon had been warm, but now the sun vanished behind a cloud and Connor found himself shivering in his thin T-shirt. 'Perhaps we should all put more clothes on,' he said to the others when they had parked their bikes. 'It's getting chilly.'

'If you ask me, this place is creepy,' said Abby, looking at the silent farm buildings. 'I'm *glad* you don't live here, Andy.'

The farmhouse was grey and square. Its curtained windows stared blankly at them. It stood like an island in the middle of a sea of gravel.

'It wasn't like this when it was a proper farm,'

said Andy, but Connor could see that he was disappointed.

'It's a great spot though,' he commented. 'Really wild and lonely.'

'You can see on the map,' said Toby. 'There's nothing beyond the farm but mountains and moors. That's why the road turns back and goes along the other side and then over that hill into the next valley.'

'I think Abby's right,' said Priya. 'I don't like it here much.'

'Let's get moving,' Connor suggested. 'I'm feeling cold. The climb to the campsite will warm us up.'

He was right about that. The road crossed two fields and then turned to the right. They passed an old road sign leaning sideways. There was a picture of a hill on it.

'It says one in five,' said Priya. 'What does that mean?'

'It means it goes up one metre in every five it goes along,' Jay told her.

'It means we'll probably have to get off and walk,' added Abby.

Connor realized that they were all feeling tired. It had been a long and exciting day and it looked as if the hardest part was yet to come.

'I'm not getting off,' said Jay. 'I bet I don't have to. Just watch.'

Connor grinned. He was proud of Tiger Patrol. There was always someone who managed to lift everyone else's spirits when things were tough. They set off in a line behind Jay, with Connor bringing up the rear. Soon they were in their lowest gears and standing up on the pedals. It was easily the steepest road Connor had ever cycled up, and just when he had begun to think that he was going to make it all the way, he looked up and saw an even steeper hill ahead.

Jay was nearly at the top, with Andy and Abby not far behind him, but halfway up the steepest bit Toby began to wobble. There was a sudden shout from Jay, who had stopped right at the top.

'You're nearly there,' he yelled. 'Zigzag! There's no cars coming.'

'No,' grunted Connor, trying desperately to keep his bike moving. 'Not safe.'

But even as he said it, his bike wobbled and he found himself going sideways, and suddenly it was easier. It was far easier. He glanced back down the hill and saw that the road was clear all the way back to the bridge.

'I can see for miles,' called Jay. 'Don't worry.'

'We can do it,' said Connor. 'Come on, Priya. Go from side to side.'

'This is why roads have hairpin bends,' said Toby, ahead of them. He stood on the pedals as he turned at the side of the road, and Priya followed him.

Connor heard their shouts of triumph as they reached the top, but he was struggling now. His legs burned as he made the final turn, but somehow he found the energy to force the bike the final few metres to the top. He stopped, gasping for breath, as the other Tigers let out a cheer.

'That was awesome!' gasped Andy, lowering his camcorder. 'It looked like something out of the Tour de France!'

'And look,' said Jay. 'You can see the whole valley from here. There's that field with the cows in, just the other side of the river and the wood.'

But Connor was bent double, trying to get his breath back. He saw Priya beside him, also breathing hard. 'Brilliant, Priya,' he said when he could finally speak. 'Just think – you could hardly ride a bike six weeks ago.'

Priya smiled a very tired smile. 'Is it much further now?' she asked.

'About a mile,' said Toby, looking at his watch. 'We're going to be there in plenty of time.'

The final stretch felt easy after the gruelling climb. Connor had time to look at the view. Jay was right – the shapes of the black-and-white cows stood out boldly against the rich green of the field. 'We can't see the farm though,' he said.

'It's just on the other side of that hill,' Toby

told him. 'And here's the campsite. We've done it! Oh, *no*!'

They all stopped in the entrance to the site. Parked in front of the toilet block was a dirty green Land Rover.

'It's all right,' said Toby suddenly. 'I'm an idiot. It's not the same one. It's a different number plate, see?'

'Hi there,' said a deep voice. A tall man with short grey hair emerged from the toilet block and smiled at them. 'I'm Graham Oak, and you must be Tiger Patrol. You're early! We haven't had many visitors yet this year and there are no more bookings for tonight. You'll have the place to yourselves.'

The Tigers followed him as he showed them the toilet and the shower. 'It's pretty basic, but Dr Sutcliff said you'd like it like that.'

'My dad's not here, is he?' said Connor, looking at the Land Rover again, as if he expected his dad to suddenly appear from the back.

Mr Oak laughed. 'No. He arrived at my place earlier and came over to check the site. He asked me to make sure that you're all in one piece and haven't got yourselves into any scrapes. He said you have a talent for that kind of thing.'

Connor thought that his dad had been saying way too much. He realized that Mr Oak was looking at his face. 'I fell off my bike,' he explained. 'I'm fine now, honestly.'

'Don't worry,' the farmer laughed. 'I saw you all come up the hill. If you can manage that, then there's not too much the matter with you. Now give me a hand to unload the Land Rover. I've got some firewood in here for you, but you'll need to chop it.'

They all helped to carry the logs to the bottom corner of the campsite. 'I should have thought,' said Toby. 'I didn't bring an axe.'

They all began to laugh. Toby usually had everything they needed in his rucksack.

'It's because you've got panniers,' Jay said. 'You didn't have enough room.'

'I would have put one in if I'd thought,' Toby said.

'Just as well you didn't, I'd say,' said Mr Oak. 'Now look, Connor – I've put a chopping block and a sawing horse over here. There's a small axe and a bow saw for you to use. Your dad told me some of you have been trained to use them properly . . .'

'Me and Abby and Toby,' Connor said. They'd all learned at Camp the previous summer, but Andy had been too busy taking pictures and had missed his turn.

'OK, then. You'd better get started cutting this lot up. I told your dad I'd supervise you while you're doing it. Then I've got a few jobs to do up at the cottage there. I'm doing it up, you see, to rent out to holidaymakers. Don't worry – I'll keep out of your way.'

'That's just stupid!' Jay burst out when Mr Oak had gone. 'Why do you need training to cut up a few bits of wood?'

'It's what we have to do,' said Connor. 'You'll

131

have to come to Camp in the summer holidays and then you'll know the rules—'

'I know what to do now,' interrupted Jay. 'I'm good with tools and things. You know I am.'

'Connor's right,' Toby said firmly. 'We have to follow the rules, Jay. You know that's how it works. Come on, let's start putting our tent up.'

Connor looked gratefully at his APL. He didn't have the energy for an argument. Even though Jay had been in the Scouts for more than six months now, there were still some things he just didn't get, and it didn't take much to make him lose his temper. 'I'll go first,' he said to the others. 'Can you start on our tent, Andy?'

Just for a second Connor thought Andy was going to want to start making movies, but then he grinned and began unhooking the panniers from his and Connor's bikes. 'I bet I have the tent up before you've chopped ten of those logs,' he said.

'You're on.'

Connor lost, but it was a close-run thing. By

the time he had finished, all three tents were up. Abby and Priya had finished first and were already unrolling their sleeping bags. Andy had just pushed in the final peg as Connor split the last log. Ten minutes later everyone's possessions were neatly stowed in their tents and Toby was getting ready to light the fire.

'Lend us your knife, Connor,' he said. 'I want to try and light it without any paper. I'll shave some bits off this dry stick and then there's plenty of small stuff to use.'

Connor handed over the Swiss Army knife that had once belonged to his grandfather. The blade, as Toby knew, was razor-sharp, and he soon had a good pile of curling white shavings. He struck a match and the flame took hold instantly. Soon a small blaze was crackling in the centre of the fire pit.

'Very good,' said Mr Oak, looking around the neat encampment approvingly. 'What's that pile of earth for?'

'Well, we didn't have a bucket,' said Toby. 'But

I brought a folding shovel so we made a heap of earth in case we have to put the fire out in a hurry.'

'You know what?' said Mr Oak cheerfully. 'I think I'll be able to report back that you're just about the most organized campers I've ever seen. Have a good night!'

He jumped back into his Land Rover and drove away. The sound of the engine faded until all that was left was the distant sound of the river and the chatter of birdsong.

'At last,' said Connor, 'we're properly on our own.'

CHAPTER 12

Priya sat on an upturned log beside the fire and watched as Connor carefully added wood until they had a good blaze going. The others were chatting happily about the events of the day.

'I was thinking of joining that mountain-biking club with Jez,' said Jay. 'But after today I'm sure it's road racing I really want to do. Only I'd need to get a proper road bike, and they cost a lot of money.'

'You'd have to get all the gear too,' laughed Toby. 'Those tight shorts and coloured tops.'

'Maybe,' said Jay seriously. 'Mum says she'll give me extra pocket money to help with the gardening and Dad says he'll pay me to clean the car. I'm going to save up.'

'Now I'm really worried,' said Connor, smiling. 'What if you don't have time for Scouts?'

'Of course I will. After all, I still have to learn how to chop wood and light a fire, don't I?'

'It's not Connor's fault,' began Toby, but Jay shook his head and started to laugh.

'I know that,' he said. 'I was just winding you up. And I would never have got the fire going as well as that. Can I put some more wood on?'

'No.' Andy held up a hand as Jay picked up a couple of sticks. 'We have to let it die down now.'

'Don't worry,' said Toby. 'There's plenty to do, Jay. You can go and wash the spuds. We're only letting the fire die down a bit so we can cook them in the embers. Abby knows what to do with them. She'll show you.'

'I didn't think I'd be hungry after that massive late lunch,' said Andy. 'But actually, I think I am!'

'Well, we definitely have to cook an evening meal,' Connor added. 'It's part of the challenge. I bet we'll manage to eat it.'

'You use a lot of energy, cycling,' Jay told them. 'More than you'd think. It always makes you extra hungry.'

Abby and Jay went off to wash the potatoes. Across the valley the sun was dipping closer to the hilltops and the fields on the far side of the river were already in shadow. Somewhere in the distance, sheep were bleating. There was a long bubbling cry from somewhere in the valley bottom.

'It's a curlew!' exclaimed Andy. 'It's coming this way – look!'

Just for a second, the bird was above their heads, and Priya saw the pointed wings and long curved beak. Then it was gone. A cold breeze had sprung up and she pulled her jacket more tightly around her, glad of the warmth from the fire. She told herself not to think about the night. She was here now. There was nothing she could do.

A log collapsed into the fire in a shower of sparks. 'Perfect,' said Connor, with a glance at her. 'Come on, Priya. Let's get the foil ready to wrap the spuds. We have to prick them all over first and rub some salt in. They'll take about an hour. Toby, can you saw up some more wood?'

Jay and Abby returned with the potatoes, and at once Connor asked them to check the bikes over. Priya could see that Connor was making sure everyone was busy. It was clever, she thought as she rubbed the salt into the potato skins. Jay loved fixing bikes, and it stopped him getting annoyed about the things he couldn't do. She suddenly thought that maybe one day she'd be able to do what Connor was doing. Maybe *she* could be a PL. Then she laughed at herself. She wasn't even sure she could get through one night in a tent. She had a long way to go before she could become a PL.

'What's the joke?' asked Connor, wrapping the final spud in foil.

'Nothing,' Priya replied. 'What do we do now?'

'We bury them under here,' he told her.

Priya realized that he had let the fire die down

almost to nothing. Now he took a stick and excavated a pit in the embers, before placing the potatoes in the centre. Priya helped, and then they covered the foil parcels over and Connor placed a few more sticks on top. 'We need to keep the fire going,' he said, 'but we don't want a roaring blaze.'

An hour later Connor and Toby raked the potatoes out of the embers and left them in their foil at the edge of the fire while they built up the fire a little before quickly heating cans of sausage and beans in a billy-can. Then they spooned the steaming mixture onto everyone's plates. The low sun had vanished behind a line of dark clouds and the fire glowed brighter. Priya realized that Jay had been right. She was really hungry. She pulled at the foil around her potato with her fingers.

'Careful,' Toby warned her. 'They'll be hot.'

She peeled back the foil gingerly and then juggled the potato onto her plate and cut through the crispy skin to the fluffy inside. It smelled delicious, but before she could take a bite Andy stopped her.

'That's the most perfect spud I've ever seen,' he said. 'I have to take a picture!'

The Tigers all groaned, but Andy insisted. When he'd finished, silence fell as they all tucked into their food. The sun found a narrow gap between the clouds and the hilltop, and a sudden gleam of orange light lit up the faces of the Tigers, like a spotlight on a stage.

'This is the best thing we've ever done,' said Toby. 'It's a proper adventure.'

Then the sun dipped below the skyline. Connor put more sticks on the fire and blew on the embers. Flames flickered upwards and the Tigers sat contentedly as the warmth of the blaze spread outwards.

'I'm really stuffed,' said Abby. 'I'll probably have to crawl into the tent.'

Andy looked around. 'It's nearly dark. We could tell ghost stories.'

'No,' said Abby quickly, looking at Priya.

'Hey, Priya, you know lots of good stories, don't you? Like the ones you told those kids when we were stuck in the snowstorm.'

'Cool,' said Connor. 'Go on, Priya. Tell us those stories your dad used to tell you.'

The others nodded their agreement. Priya was surprised, and felt a little awkward, but she looked at her friends sitting around the fire, miles from anywhere, and suddenly she thought of Rama and his wife, Sita, and his brother, Lakshman, exiled in the forest. She began to tell the others about them. When she described how Sita had loved living in the hut in the forest because of the light that shone from the foreheads of the two brothers, Toby laughed and pulled his head-torch out of his pocket.

'We can be like Rama and Lakshman . . .' He put the torch on his head and switched it on. 'We can be superheroes!'

Connor shook his head. 'Don't waste the batteries,' he said. 'We might need them. Go on, Priya. Tell us about the monsters.'

Priya enjoyed herself. She described Rama killing fourteen thousand demons and killing their leader with a fiery arrow. Then she paused. 'There's a lot more,' she said. 'It goes on and on.'

'It's brilliant,' said Jay. 'It's kind of like a computer game.'

'Only better . . .' Abby yawned. 'Thanks, Priya.'

Priya found that she was yawning too. They all were.

'OK, then,' said Connor. 'It's time to turn in. We'll cover the fire with earth. If we're lucky, it'll still be alight in the morning.'

Priya and Abby went to the shower block to brush their teeth. The fluorescent light was dazzling and Priya screwed up her eyes.

'Are you OK?' Abby asked her.

'I think so,' she said. Telling the story had made her feel much calmer. 'My dad used to tell me those stories at bedtime. I did dream about monsters sometimes, but Rama and Sita always got rid of them.'

As they made their way back over grass that was wet with dew, they saw the shadows thrown onto the tent walls by the boys' torches. 'They look like monsters,' said Abby.

Priya laughed. 'I'm not scared of *them*,' she said.

Abby unzipped the tent and crawled inside, taking her shoes off and leaving them in the entrance. 'We have to be careful not to get anything wet inside the tent,' she said. 'And look – I brought this.'

Priya put her head inside. Something was glowing in Abby's hand.

'It's a night-light,' Abby told her. 'We can put it in the entrance; then if we wake up in the night, we'll be able to see.'

Abby quickly changed into a pair of joggers and a T-shirt, then slipped into her sleeping bag.

'I don't know how you did that.' Priya was struggling to pull her pyjamas over her head in the tiny space.

'Careful!' warned Abby. 'Don't push the inner tent against the fly sheet.'

'It's OK,' said Priya. 'It's all dry.'

'I know, but you have to get used to not doing it. In the morning there'll be condensation all over the inside of the fly sheet. Just make yourself as small as you can. There, you've done it.'

Priya folded her uniform neatly and put it at the foot of her sleeping bag, then wriggled inside and lay on her back.

'Goodnight, everyone,' Connor called from his tent.

There was a chorus of sleepy 'goodnights', and then silence. The night-light glowed gently beside Priya's head. She lay on her back and closed her eyes. Abby was breathing deeply and Priya realized that she must have fallen asleep instantly. This wasn't as bad as she'd expected. Just what her dad had predicted. She could hear his voice now, telling her bedtime stories . . . something about monkeys . . .

* * *

Priya woke with a start, her heart beating fast. Something had disturbed her but she wasn't sure what. Abby was still sleeping quietly beside her, and the night-light glowed, but now she could see things inside the tent, and she realized that the moon must have risen. She took a deep breath, trying to calm herself, but then she heard something rustling outside. *It's nothing*, she told herself grimly. *It's a hedgehog, or a mole. It's something nice and harmless.*

The sound died away, and everything was quiet once more. But not completely. There was Abby's gentle breathing. Someone coughed in one of the other tents. It sounded like Toby. And then there was another sound – a deep throbbing that was growing steadily louder. Just for a second a bright light flashed across the tent and a car drove past the campsite, followed by another.

Priya was surprised, and now she was completely awake. They'd only seen a couple of cars all day, and now two had come past together. Although, now she thought about it, one of them must have been a truck, or a tractor, because its engine had sounded much too deep for a car.

She looked at the dark hump beside her that was Abby, fast asleep. The noise didn't seem to have woken anyone else. She could still hear it, and she imagined the two cars, or whatever they were, reaching the foot of the hill and crossing the bridge by Greystone Farm. She heard the rattle as they crossed the cattle grid on the far side, so now they must be going along on the other side of the valley.

For a while the sound didn't change and then, quite suddenly, it stopped. Priya wondered about that. Maybe they'd stopped at the Joneses' farm. Maybe the farmer had been out visiting someone in the other valley. Whatever it was, she was going to take to look.

Very quietly, so as not to wake Abby, she unfastened the zip of the inner tent, then reached up to open the damp fly sheet. She pulled back the flap and realized she could see the whole valley, blue and black and silver in the moonlight. Directly opposite, on the far side of the valley, she saw two pairs of headlights, not moving. As she watched, the lights went out.

Then it hit her.

They were sheep stealers. Rustlers! They had to be. It couldn't possibly be Mr Jones. Why would he have two vehicles? Why would he park there with the lights out? She knew she was right.

She wriggled back inside the tent and shook Abby's shoulder. 'Abby! Wake up!'

'What is it? What's going on?'

'Abby, something's happening. On the other side of the valley . . . I think they're stealing sheep.'

Abby groaned. 'It's the middle of the night. I'm asleep.'

'We have to do something,' Priya said. 'We have to tell the farmer. Abby, wake up!'

She shook Abby again, and this time Abby emerged from her sleeping bag rubbing her eyes. 'What time is it?' she asked. 'You'd better not be making this up.'

Priya looked at her watch. 'It's two in the morning,' she said. 'I can't believe the truck didn't wake you up. Have you got your binoculars?'

Abby grunted and got the binoculars out of her bag. Priya pulled on her shoes and went outside. Seconds later, Abby joined her.

'Show me,' she whispered. 'Where did you see them?'

Priya pointed, and heard a sharp intake of breath from Abby.

'You're right,' she breathed. 'There's a big lorry, and a four-by-four. It could be the one we saw this afternoon. There are men . . . I can see three – no, four. They're in the field and they've got dogs. We'll have to wake the others. Those are Mr Jones's sheep. We have to warn him. We have to get to his farm as fast as we can.'

CHAPTER 13

Connor was dreaming. He was cycling uphill as fast as he could and something was chasing him. He didn't know what it was, but he knew that he didn't want it to catch him. Someone was calling his name, but he couldn't answer. The front wheel of his bike crashed into a pothole and he was falling. Someone grabbed him and held on . . .

'Connor, wake up! You have to wake up! Andy, you too!'

Someone was shaking Connor's shoulder hard, and now a bright light flashed in his eyes. 'Point that thing somewhere else,' he said. 'What is it? What's the matter?'

The light disappeared and he saw a dark shape kneeling in the entrance of his tent. Beside him,

Andy rolled over in his sleeping bag and asked, 'Abby? What are you doing?'

Connor rubbed his eyes and shook his head, trying to wake up. Abby was saying something but it didn't make much sense.

'Just listen, can't you?' she said impatiently. 'There are men on the other side of the valley. They've got a big truck and they're going to steal the sheep. We have to stop them.'

'OK,' said Connor. 'Calm down, Abby. Let me get out of my sleeping bag and I'll take a look.'

'I suppose we'll all have to get up,' Andy sighed. 'This had better not be one of your jokes, Abby.'

'As if I would,' she said indignantly. 'And anyway, it was Priya who spotted them, wasn't it, Priya?'

'They're still there,' Priya said as Connor pulled on a fleece and jumped out of the tent. She was watching intently through Abby's binoculars. 'There are a lot of sheep quite high up on the hillside and I think that's where they're heading.'

Connor took out his own binoculars and looked for himself. He saw the dark shapes of figures moving slowly up through a field, and then a fast-moving black dot that must be a dog, heading off to one side, well away from the scattered sheep, which were still some way off. 'They must be thieves,' he said to Toby.

Toby and Jay had both crawled sleepily out of their tent to join the others.

'You're right – a farmer wouldn't move sheep in the middle of the night,' Toby agreed. 'We should call the police.'

'But we can't,' said Priya. 'There's no phone signal here, and no phone box.'

'What about Mr Oak's farm?' said Andy. 'How far is that?'

'It's nearly ten kilometres away,' said Connor, thinking fast. 'By the time we got there and the police arrived, they'd be long gone.'

'We could climb up that hill and try to get a

signal on the phone,' suggested Toby, pointing at the dark bulk of hillside rising behind them. 'It's what your dad said we ought to do in a desperate emergency.'

'He also said the signal's hit and miss,' Connor replied. 'It could take a while.'

'Those *are* Mr Jones's sheep, aren't they?' asked Priya. 'If they take all of them, he might have to stop being a farmer. His farm would end up like your great-grandad's, Andy. A place for holiday people.'

'We'll have to tell him then,' said Jay. 'It's the only thing to do. We have to go now.'

'I think Jay's right,' Connor told the others. 'But it's not that easy. We'd have to get past their truck without them seeing us.'

'Maybe it would be good if they did see us,' suggested Andy. 'Maybe they'd just take off.'

'That's no good. We're not going to take any risks. Didn't you say there was a footpath, Toby – through that field with the cows in?'

Toby was already looking at the map. 'We

can cycle to here,' he said, pointing. 'Then there's a path down to the river, all the way along there, and up through the fields. I'm sure we could do it.'

'All right,' said Connor, 'but we don't have much time. Everyone get ready as fast as you can . . .'

As he put on his helmet, he had a brief moment of doubt. Were they doing the right thing? Was there anything else they could do? One thing was certain: they couldn't just do nothing. Priya was right. Mr and Mrs Jones could lose their farm because of this. If they could only get there in time!

He looked around. They were all ready, standing by their bikes. 'OK,' he said. 'We'll go in single file. Toby, you lead. You know where we have to stop, don't you?'

Toby nodded. There was a sudden flash as Abby switched her front light on. 'Turn it off!' said Connor. 'We have to do this without lights. If we can see them from here, they'd be able to see us too. If a car does come, then we'll just have to stop and turn them on, but this moonlight is bright enough to see by. Just be careful, Toby.'

They wheeled their bikes down the gravel slope to the gate and Toby set off down the road. Connor brought up the rear and found that he could see quite well enough to ride safely. Once more he felt a stab of doubt. This was actually against the law, but if they were going to stop the sheep rustlers, there was no way they could ride through the valley with their lights on. He wondered what his grandpa would say, and immediately heard his voice in his head: *Decisions aren't always black and white, Connor. Life isn't like that. It's not easy working out what to do in a tricky situation, but that's the Leader's job. And once you've made your decision, for goodness' sake don't waste time worrying if you've done the right thing. Do what you've decided to do as well as you can.*

Suddenly Connor had to concentrate hard as, one by one, the other Tigers disappeared over the brow of the very steep hill. He was relieved to see that they had all applied their brakes and were descending carefully. At the bottom Toby accelerated away and the others were strung out in a line as they pedalled fast towards the bridge, their tyres hissing on the tarmac. They passed the buildings of Greystone Farm, dark and silent on their right; then they were over the bridge, with just a glimpse of the water foaming below them, before they started climbing again.

Connor glanced at the luminous dial of his watch. Only five minutes so far, but now they had to pedal three kilometres uphill. Priya seemed to be slowing down. 'Are you OK?' he asked her, anxiously watching the others pull ahead.

'My bike won't go very fast – I don't know what's the matter with it,' she said. 'But don't worry about me. It's not far now. The others will need you.'

Priya was right. Even though Connor didn't like leaving her, it was more important to make sure that none of the others did anything impulsive. He knew what Abby was like.

He changed gear and leaned on the pedals, then felt a twinge from the muscles in his thigh. He'd forgotten about his fall, but now his leg began to hurt and he was forced to go more slowly. Even so, it only took him a few minutes to reach the point where they had agreed to stop. The other Tigers were lifting their bikes over a gate.

'I thought we should put them out of the way,' Toby said. 'The path starts about a hundred metres along there.' He pointed along the road.

'Let's go carefully,' Connor said. 'It's just possible that we'll be in view for a while before we reach the path. We'd better stay close to the wall on that side, and keep our heads down.'

'But where's Priya?' asked Abby.

'She was right behind me. She thought there might be something wrong with her bike, but she'll be here any minute, even if she has to push.'

'I'll go back and check,' offered Jay. 'If there's

something wrong, I can fix it.' He leaped onto his bike and tore off back down the lane.

Priya had carried on for only a few metres after Connor had left her before realizing that something was badly wrong with her front wheel. She stopped and leaned the bike against a wall, then crouched down for a closer look. She had a flat tyre!

Priya knew that she had to make a decision quickly. She could leave the bike here and run to catch up with the others, but she might need the bike later. Or she could push it up the road and fix the puncture later. Or she could do it now. That would be the best thing, if only she could manage it. It was lucky it was her front tyre.

Once she had made her decision she acted quickly, but systematically, just as Jay had shown her. She took her toolkit out of her saddlebag, then upended the bike, slackened off the brake and removed the wheel. She slipped a tyre lever under the rim of the tyre, then another, then a third. The tyre popped off easily. So far so good. She removed the old inner tube and felt round the inside of the tyre, trying to find what had caused the puncture. Something pricked her finger and she nearly cried out. It was a long thorn. She grabbed it with her fingernails and pulled it out of the tyre, then quickly fitted the new inner tube from her bag.

How long had she been? she wondered anxiously as she put the tyre back on and inflated the tube. She couldn't have done it any faster. An owl screeched in the dark woods away to her left, but she hardly noticed as she raced to fix the wheel in place and reset the brake. There! It was done. She packed her tools away and jumped back on the bike, pedalling furiously up the hill. She was coming round the final bend when she saw a dark shadow moving rapidly towards her. The shadow slewed to a halt and she saw Jay standing astride his bike.

'Are you OK?' he asked. 'What happened?'

'I'm fine,' she replied in a low voice. 'A

puncture, that's all. I fixed it. Why have you stopped? We have to get back to the others.'

'You must have done that fast,' said Jay as they headed back up the road together.

Priya heard a note of admiration in his voice and felt pleased. 'I just did what you showed me,' she told him.

'Shhh!' Jay warned her. 'We're there.'

Connor was very relieved when Jay reappeared almost at once, with Priya beside him. 'Well done,' he whispered to her when he heard what had happened. 'Let's get moving.'

On their right was a low grassy bank topped by a drystone wall. It cast a dark shadow onto the road and they made their way forward as quietly as they could. Connor could hear the roar of the river away to their left beyond the fields and the black outline of the trees. Suddenly Toby halted. He was pointing up to the right and ahead. Connor saw sheep moving high up on the hillside, and heard their nervous bleating. And there, not four hundred metres ahead of them, he saw the truck. It was facing towards them now, its windshield glittering in the moonlight. 'They must have turned round in the field entrance,' Toby hissed. 'They'll go back the way they came in so they don't have to go past the farms along the valley.'

'Stay in the shadows,' Connor whispered urgently as Jay tried to see past Toby. 'There might be someone in the truck.'

'There's the start of the footpath,' said Toby, indicating a stile on the opposite side of the road. 'If someone's there, they'll see us when we cross.'

'Give me your binoculars,' Jay said to Toby. 'I'll wriggle forward and get a better angle. It's just the moonlight shining on the windscreen.'

Before Connor had a chance to say anything, Jay had taken the binoculars and was creeping forward along the verge. He paused, looked through the glasses and then moved a few metres further. After a few moments he turned and crawled back towards them. 'It's OK,' he said.

'There's no one in the cab. Most likely they're all away up there.'

'Right then,' said Connor. 'Let's move. Across the road quickly, one at a time. You go first, Jay.'

One by one they sprinted across the moonlit road and into the shelter of the gateway on the far side. When Connor joined them, Jay was gazing through the binoculars up at the hillside. 'We'll never make it to the farm in time,' he said. 'They're rounding them up already. By the time Mr Jones has called the police they'll have gone.'

'They'll still have a chance to catch them,' Connor pointed out. 'There's only one road out of the valley.'

'But as soon as they're over the hill there are dozens of routes they could take,' Toby muttered glumly. 'Jay's right. They're going to get away.'

'We could stop them,' said Jay.

There was a moment's silence. 'What, stand in front of the truck?' asked Andy. 'We haven't got time for this. Let's go.'

'That's not what I mean. It's simple. All we

have to do is let their tyres down and they won't be able to go anywhere.'

Connor hesitated. It might be possible. 'Do you know how to do it?' he asked Jay.

'It's easy. The valves are the same as the ones on our bikes. You press down the little spike in the middle and the air comes out. We only need to do one. I bet it takes ages to change one of those wheels.'

'He's right,' said Toby. 'It shouldn't be difficult. We can creep along the side of the truck. One of us can keep watch, and if anyone comes, we'll slip away. As long as we watch carefully, they'll never know how it's happened.'

'All right,' said Connor. 'We'll do it.' Toby was the most sensible person he knew, and if he thought Jay's idea would work, then that made all the difference. He couldn't bear to think that the thieves might escape. 'You and Abby can go to the farm,' he told Priya. 'Andy, you go with them. Hurry.'

'Here's the map,' Toby said, handing it to

Abby. 'It's really simple. You follow this path to the river and then follow it until it bends round to the left. You'll probably see the cows. You go straight up through their field, and then it's only a kilometre to the farm.'

'Is that the only way?' asked Abby.

'Oh, come on,' Andy scoffed. 'You're not really scared of them, are you?'

Abby looked at Priya and hesitated. 'Of course not,' she said. 'I'll be OK. And anyway, we have to do it for the Joneses. Let's get going.'

The two girls and Andy hurried off and were soon lost to sight.

'All right then,' said Connor, trying not to show how shaky he was feeling. 'What are they doing up there, Jay?'

'I'm not sure. The sheep are still in that top field, and I think the men are too.'

'Let's get as close as we can while we're in the shelter of this wall. Then we'll go round on the opposite side of the truck so that they can't see us from where they are. OK?'

The other two nodded, and they all moved along the road in the narrow patch of shadow. A couple of minutes later they'd reached the truck. It towered over them, and they could hear the quiet ticking of cooling metal. There was a stink of diesel and disinfectant. The back of the truck was level with a field gate that stood open, and there was a barrier between the back of the truck and the wall.

'They're going to herd them straight through the gate and into the truck,' whispered Toby. 'What now?'

Connor pointed, and they made their way round to the front of the truck. The far side was in shadow.

'I'll start letting the air out,' said Jay, kneeling beside an enormous tyre.

'OK,' said Connor, his heart beating fast. 'Toby, go that way a bit, along the road. Flash your torch three times if you see them coming back. I'll keep a lookout here.'

Toby melted away beside the wall. The hiss of

air escaping from the tyre sounded incredibly loud to Connor. 'What if they hear?' he muttered to Jay.

'They're miles away,' he replied.

'How long is this going to take?'

'It's a big tyre,' said Jay. 'Don't worry. Keep your eye on Toby.'

Connor waited and watched. His heartbeat thumped in his ears. An owl hooted in the valley and he wondered about the others. How soon would they reach the farm? And when they did, what would happen then?

CHAPTER 14

Priya kept her eyes on Andy's back as he walked quickly along the edge of the first field. At the end, she could see the dark line of a hedge. 'Are you sure we can get through?' she asked Andy.

'It's marked as a footpath,' he replied, 'so there must be a stile or something. Don't waste breath on talking. We have to walk three kilometres as fast as we possibly can.'

'Well, couldn't we run this bit?' Priya suggested. 'We can see perfectly well. It might not be so easy in the woods.'

'She's right,' Abby said. 'Go on, Andy. Not fast, just jogging, OK?'

Andy set off again. The grass was tussocky and wet, and Priya found that she had to lift her feet high to avoid stumbling. A couple of minutes of jogging brought them to the hedge.

'It's not a stile, it's a gate,' Abby said. 'Open it, quick.'

'I can't see how . . .' Andy was fumbling with some kind of chain.

'Just climb over it,' said Abby. Priya put her hand on the top of the gate, but Abby stopped her. 'Not there,' she said. 'If you have to climb over, you do it by the hinge. Like this. That way you won't damage the gate.'

She put her foot on the bottom bar of the gate and vaulted neatly over the top. Priya climbed carefully over behind her and Andy followed. They jogged on along the edge of the field, and this time found a stile at the end. Beyond a barbed-wire fence the path led into the darkness under the trees.

'I can hear the river,' Priya said. 'It's really loud.'

Andy looked back towards the road. 'Once we're in the shelter of the trees we can switch our head-torches on,' he said. 'The path goes through this wood to the river and then follows it for nearly two kilometres. After that we go straight uphill to the farm.'

They moved under the trees. The moonlight filtered down through the young leaves, casting dappled shadows of blue and silver on the ground. 'It's beautiful,' murmured Priya, catching sight of the glittering water of the river a short distance away.

'Never mind that,' said Andy. 'Switch on your torch and let's go.'

His own torch sprang into life, and suddenly all Priya could see was the bright light glaring from his forehead. Everything around him was black. She couldn't even see the trees any more. She switched on her own torch, and a narrow cone of light appeared ahead of her. Andy moved off through the trees and Priya followed un-certainly. Abby stumbled as her foot caught on a branch, and she caught hold of Priya's arm to steady herself. Ahead of them, Andy let out a sharp yell as a twig scratched his face.

'I could see better without the torch,' Priya said. 'It makes one little bit of light but it makes everything else much darker.'

'Priya's right,' agreed Abby, switching hers off. 'We'll be faster without them.'

'OK, we'll try it.' Andy turned his off too. 'Oh. Now I can't see a thing.'

'It's all right,' Priya told him. 'We just have to wait for a minute until our eyes get used to it. We dazzled ourselves, that's all.'

It didn't take long for their eyes to adjust. 'It's amazing, isn't it?' said Andy. 'I'd never have thought it could be easier to see without a torch. It might even be light enough to take a picture. I wonder—'

'Andy!' exclaimed Abby. 'Don't even think about getting your camera out. This isn't a game, you know. We have to warn Mr Jones. Give me the map. I'm going in front.'

She set off very fast, and in no time at all they had reached the river. The path turned to the right and snaked along the bank, separated from the rushing water most of the time by a narrow band of trees and bushes. The path was very muddy in places, but Abby simply squelched right through the middle of the boggy patches and Priya followed in her steps. Her feet were already soaked from walking through the wet grass, so it didn't really make much difference.

Then Abby stopped so suddenly that Priya crashed into her back. 'What is it?' she asked. Then she saw. A narrow plank crossed over a stream that was blocking their way.

'What are you waiting for?' demanded Andy, joining them.

'That plank looks rotten,' Abby said. 'I don't trust it.'

'Well, it's not a very big stream,' he pointed out. 'We can just wade through. I don't know about you, but I don't think my feet can get any wetter.'

'OK,' said Priya. 'I'll go first.'

'Priya, wait,' Abby said. 'We'd better take off our boots.'

'No way,' said Priya. 'I remember Mihir telling me about crossing streams. He learned about it in Explorer Scouts. You keep your boots on. What if there's something sharp under the water? And it's easier to keep your footing. We can empty the water out afterwards if we need to.'

Priya stepped determinedly into the water. She gasped as she felt its icy grip on her ankles, then took a step towards the middle. The water came up to her knees, but the gravelly bottom was firm. She climbed quickly onto the opposite bank. 'It's easy,' she said. 'Come on.'

The others followed her across the stream. 'We can't stop to empty our boots,' said Abby. 'This is already taking much more time than I thought.'

'It hasn't been that long,' said Andy, looking at his watch. 'Only ten minutes so far. It just *seems* like ages. Keep walking, Priya. I reckon it's your turn to be leader.'

Priya walked on quickly, her boots squelching loudly with every step. The woods were full of damp smells of wild garlic and leaves and growing things, and she realized that even though they were on a very serious mission, she was enjoying every minute of it. Then she thought of the three boys trying to delay the thieves and remembered the tall black shape of the truck with its shiny windows, and she put on an extra spurt of speed.

They followed the riverside path for another ten minutes until it turned sharply to the left. 'This must be the place,' Andy said. 'Look, the river's turning as well. Hold on – let's check the map.'

They all leaned over the map and Andy flashed his torch on it. 'We're here,' he said, pointing. 'There'll be a gate or a stile somewhere on our right.'

'We'd better walk slowly,' Priya suggested. 'You're right, Andy. The trees end there, fifty metres away, I think. So the beginning of the path should be about a hundred and fifty metres from there. Let's say if we walk four hundred metres and still haven't found it, we'll know we've gone too far.'

'Good thinking,' said Andy. 'But we have to find it first time. We can all count our steps.'

The Tigers had had plenty of practice estimating distances by counting their steps when they'd been orienteering on the moors.

Priya concentrated hard as the sound of the river faded behind them. 'That's it,' she said. 'I make it two hundred.'

The others stopped behind her. 'Yes!' she exclaimed. 'Over there! There's a gate and a signpost.'

An indistinct path led across a patch of grass towards the gate. Before they reached it they all halted.

'What's that noise?' asked Andy. 'It's really weird!'

Priya heard a strange tearing sound coming from the field ahead – then a loud, deep belch, and she laughed. 'It's the cows,' she said, moving forward to lean on the gate. 'Look, they're eating in the middle of the night!'

It was a strange scene that met their eyes. The

black-and-white shapes of the cows seemed to be floating above the layer of mist that rose from the wet grass and curled around their legs. Their heads dipped into the mist, tearing at the grass, chewing and swallowing.

'Wow,' said Andy. 'I never knew they did that. They're like ghost cows.'

'Neither did I,' murmured Abby faintly.

'It's OK,' said Priya. 'Just look at them, Abby. They're much too solid and noisy to be ghosts, and they're not the least bit interested in us. All they care about is eating. I'll go first.'

She climbed over the gate – at the hinge end – and set off along the path, which ran straight across the field. The cows ignored her completely as Abby and Andy followed her over the gate. Priya walked steadily on as the mist swirled around her. The field began to slope upwards and eventually she reached a stile. She looked back and a single cow raised her head and stared at the three Tigers as they climbed over.

'Thanks, Priya,' said Abby as they jogged up

the hill towards the road. 'I don't think I could have done that if you hadn't led the way.'

'We're there,' said Andy excitedly as they went through an open gate and found themselves standing on the silver ribbon of road. 'We can run now. We're going to make it.'

'No, we're not,' said Abby. 'Look!'

Andy looked where she was pointing. 'What? There's nothing . . .'

'That's the field where the sheep were,' Priya told him. 'They've gone.'

'We'll just have to hope that the others have sorted the truck,' he said grimly. 'Come on, run. As fast as we can.'

Andy and Abby soon pulled away from Priya. They were easily the fastest runners in Tiger Patrol and Priya knew she couldn't expect to keep up, but she carried on grimly, pushing her legs as fast as they'd go. The road turned a corner and then ran straight for a while; she turned into the straight bit just in time to see the other two disappear up the farm track. She had just started up the track when she heard the sudden uproar of barking dogs. She found Andy and Abby in the farmyard, frozen against the barn, with two of Mr Jones's dogs standing in front of them, snarling through bared teeth.

Priya backed away. Across the yard a door opened and yellow light streamed across the cobbles. Mr Jones was silhouetted in the doorway. 'Who are you, and what do you think you're doing?' he shouted.

Andy and Abby were too frightened to speak.

'It's us,' called Priya, but her voice came out like a whisper. She cleared her throat and tried again. 'It's Priya,' she said. 'And Abby and Andy. The Scouts from this afternoon. There are men on the hill. They're stealing your sheep.'

'What?' Mr Jones stepped into the yard and shone an incredibly bright torch in Priya's face. Then the beam swung round and fell on Abby and Andy. 'Well, I'll be . . . What on earth do you think you're doing, creeping around here in the middle of the night? Here, Bess. Here, Jenny.'

The two dogs backed off, still suspicious.

'We came to warn you,' said Abby, taking a deep breath. 'They've got a truck and they're rounding up the sheep on the hill. But I think we're too late. We came by the river and it took too long and they're going to get away.'

The farmer strode across the yard. He shone the torch on the Scouts' wet clothes. 'Are you sure?' he asked, then paused. 'Where are your friends?'

'They stayed behind,' said Priya. 'It was Jay's idea. They were going to let down the tyres on the truck so it couldn't get away.'

'Good Lord!' exclaimed Mr Jones. 'Did you hear that, Gladys?' he asked his wife, who was bustling across the yard towards them. 'I've got to get down there. I don't believe it. Letting down their tyres! And you three coming all this way. You call the police, love,' he said to his wife. 'I'm going to take the dogs and see if I can't round up some crooks.'

'But we want to come,' said Andy.

'Nonsense,' said Mrs Jones. 'You're soaked, all three of you, and it's not safe. They can be very dangerous, these thieves. They've attacked farmers before now when they've tried to stop them.' She turned to her husband. 'You be careful, Thomas, won't you! It might be better to wait for the police . . .' She looked at the three Scouts again. 'I just hope your friends have had the sense to keep out of their way. Now, you come inside and we'll get you warm.'

As they reached the farmhouse door, Priya heard the sound of an engine. They all turned and saw Mr Jones on the quad bike, turning out of the yard. His five dogs followed like black shadows. Priya shivered. She had seen the look that had passed between the farmer and his wife.

The others were in real danger, and there was nothing that she or Abby or Andy could do.

CHAPTER 15

'Why is it taking so long?' asked Connor.

'I told you,' said Jay in a low voice. 'There's a lot of air to come out, and anyway, we've hardly been any time at all. What's happening up on the hill? Can you see?'

'No,' replied Connor, after edging round to the front of the truck and risking a quick glance up at the hillside. 'We have to trust Toby. He'll have found a place where he can see what's going on.'

'Well, you should keep watching for his signal,' said Jay. 'Don't keep asking me how long this'll take. It makes me nervous.'

'OK.' Connor looked at his watch and saw that Jay was right. They'd only been here for a couple of minutes, but it seemed like hours.

'Sorry, Jay. I'll go round the back. If Toby signals I'll come and tell you.'

He made his way along the side of the truck. As he did so, he inspected the hedge on his left, searching for a place to make a quick getaway if they needed to, but it looked dense and very thorny. He gazed down the road. Toby had hidden himself well. There was no sign of him in the shadows, and no flashing light.

The waiting was terrible. Connor had thought the air would come out of the tyre fast, like the air from a balloon. It certainly seemed to come out fast enough when you had a puncture on your bike. If only he had something to do. Then his eyes fell on the Land Rover. It was parked just beyond the gateway. Why shouldn't he let down one of *its* tyres? That way the men would be trapped completely. And he could do it while he watched out for Toby. He couldn't believe that they hadn't thought of it before.

Connor slipped into the shadow of the wall, then darted across the gateway before re-crossing the road into the shelter of the Land Rover. He crouched down by the front wheel, quickly checked to see if Toby was signalling, then removed the dust-cap and pressed down on the valve with his thumbnail. The air flowed out with a satisfying hiss, and after a few seconds Connor was almost sure he could see the tyre deflating. It was going to work! It was actually going down as he watched. Seconds ticked by. The front of the Land Rover slowly subsided, squashing the tyre flat. He'd done it!

'Connor!' hissed Toby urgently, grabbing his shoulder. 'I've been signalling for ages. They're coming! We have to get out of here.'

Connor felt sick. How could he have been such an idiot? He hadn't even been listening. If he had, he would have heard the low murmur of voices and the sound of dozens of hooves trotting across the field.

'Quick!' said Toby. 'Into the shadow of the wall. Then we can creep away.'

'But what about Jay?' asked Connor, his

heart thumping. 'He's still by the truck.'

'What?'

'We can't get to him now. They'll see us through the gateway.'

'I'll signal,' Toby said.

'They'll see.'

'We have to risk it. I'll give him a quick flash. I bet he's looking. He must be wondering what's happened to you.'

Almost at once Jay appeared, his face white, his hands open as if to ask what he should do. Before he could step out of the shadows, Connor gestured him back urgently. Realization dawned on him as he heard the sound of the approaching sheep. He melted back into the gloom.

'Don't worry about Jay,' Toby told Connor. 'He can take care of himself. We need to get clear ourselves. We should be able to make it back to the place I was watching from. But we have to do it right now.'

Connor nodded his agreement. Toby put a finger to his lips and pointed to the back of the

Land Rover and then across the road. Connor nodded again. Toby slipped away and Connor followed. As he crossed the road, he heard the sound of laughter very close by and froze. Toby reached up and pulled him back into the shadow of the wall. They edged along together until the curve of the road hid them from the truck, then Toby stopped.

'I found a place where you can see the fields and the truck,' he said. 'Up here.'

There was a kink in the wall where a small spur of rock jutted out from the hillside and two fields joined. They climbed up onto the rocks and looked cautiously over the top of the wall. Sheep were pouring through the open gate a hundred metres away. They heard the low voices of the men and then the clatter of hooves on the ramp that led up into the truck.

'They haven't noticed the flat tyre yet,' breathed Toby. 'Do you think Jay managed to do it?'

'He must have,' said Connor. 'Maybe they're

too busy with the sheep. I hope Jay's safe. I can't believe I was so stupid.'

'It was a good idea to let down the tyre on the Land Rover, though. And we all got away, didn't we? Look – any minute now they're going to get a big shock.'

The ramp was hauled up and the bolts at the back of the truck clanged shut. Connor made out the shapes of four men behind it, talking together. Then the group split up. Moments later they heard doors slamming and the truck's engine roared into life. The back door of the Land Rover opened and shut, moonlight glinting off the glass, and then Connor was dazzled as the lights of both vehicles blazed out. The truck began to move forward, then suddenly stopped. A door opened and they heard someone swearing angrily. Connor squeezed Toby's arm. Everything was going to plan. The other two men jumped out of the Land Rover and went round to the front of the truck. Suddenly there was a shout, and all four men began running down the road.

'He went down there!' one of them called.

'Wait!' yelled another voice. 'Maybe it's a trap.'

'They've seen Jay,' Toby whispered.

'Come on,' said Connor. 'We can let the sheep out. They'll never catch them again and they won't have a clue what's happening.'

'Cool,' said Toby. 'Let's do it.'

They sprinted forward. They caught a glimpse of three sheepdogs shut inside the Land Rover, barking furiously, then they were releasing the bolts at the back of the truck. They lowered the ramp, and sheep began spilling out onto the road. They ran everywhere, back through the open gate, either side of the Land Rover and off into the distance; some ran down the road behind the men, who instantly turned and ran back towards the truck.

'Into the field,' said Connor. 'Quick!'

Toby didn't need telling. He was already running through the gate and up the steeply sloping grass, with Connor right behind him.

They heard shouts, but neither of them looked back. And then the night air was filled with the sound of barking and snarling.

'No!' gasped Toby. 'The dogs!'

'OK,' said Connor. 'That's it. No point trying to run from them.'

'No,' said Toby. 'Look, Connor! It's not us they're after. Those are Mr Jones's dogs. Look at the white patch on that one's nose. It's Meg!'

Connor turned and looked back down the hill. The men who had been chasing them were fifty metres away but they had stopped. Two angry dogs stood between them and the boys, snarling menacingly. The men edged backwards towards the gate, huddling together and talking urgently. Each time they took a step back, the dogs moved towards them.

'Ready?' said one of the men. 'One, two, three . . .'

They ran for the gate, one pair heading towards the truck, the others towards the Land Rover, but as they reached the field entrance they skidded to a halt. One of them lost his footing and crashed to the ground, swearing loudly.

Three more dogs stood in the gateway, bared teeth white in the moonlight.

'They're herding them like sheep,' breathed Toby as the dogs moved the men slowly but surely towards the ramp and forced them up into the back of the truck. 'Where did they come from?'

'Listen . . .' said Connor. 'I bet that's Mr Jones. The others did it! They got there in time!'

The throb of an engine was approaching rapidly, and now the beams of headlights illuminated the trees in the valley. The boys ran over to the gate and saw Jay sprinting towards them up the road. He had just reached them when the quad bike came in sight, going faster than Connor would have believed possible. It screeched to a halt and Mr Jones leaped off. He shot one brief, angry glance at the men sitting in sullen silence in the back of the truck and then turned to the Scouts.

'You're all right?' he asked anxiously. 'Let me look at you . . .' He shone his torch in their faces, dazzling them. 'Well,' he said finally, his face breaking into a smile, 'I can't say it's something I'd have wanted you to do, but I'm very glad you did it.'

'Are the others OK?' asked Connor. 'They all got to the farm?'

'Oh, yes,' replied the farmer. 'They got a bit of a shock from the dogs though. I'm going to call the farm and tell Gladys what's happened. You can talk to them if you like.'

'But phones don't work here,' said Toby. 'How . . . ?'

'CB radio . . .' Mr Jones grinned as he held up the handset. 'My daughter bought it for us. It stops Gladys worrying when I'm out on the hills. She reckons I'm a reckless driver, if you can believe that.' He spoke into the radio: 'Hello, Gladys. Good news. The kids are fine and the dogs have the thieves rounded up. They're all ready to have a word with the police. Over.'

188

'I'm coming down there,' said Mrs Jones's voice from the handset. 'I want to look at those children for myself. The police will be there in fifteen minutes. They had a patrol out down the valley.' The radio went dead.

'She ought to say "Over and out" really,' said Mr Jones, shaking his head. 'I can never get her to do it properly. Now let's see what you've done to their truck.'

He walked round to the front and shone his torch downwards. The tyre was almost off the rim.

'They tried to drive away,' Jay told him. 'I couldn't believe it. I thought they'd be sure to notice when they got in. Then I poked my head out to see what was going on, and that's when they spotted me.'

'Then we let the sheep out of the back,' Connor said.

'Good job you did,' said Jay. 'But they would never have caught me. They weren't very fast. I could hear them gasping.'

A thought hit Connor. 'I'm really sorry, Mr Jones,' he said. 'Your sheep – they went everywhere.'

The farmer laughed. 'Don't worry about them,' he said as they heard the sound of an engine and saw the lights of a car approaching. 'They'll be back in the morning, and they're all marked anyway. Besides, I reckon most of them will just go back into their field.'

The car pulled up, and almost before it had stopped, Andy, Abby and Priya had leaped out and dashed over to join the other Tigers. They stared in amazement at the five dogs guarding the back of the truck.

By the time Connor had explained to them what had happened, the police had arrived on the scene and he found himself having to explain to one of the officers exactly what they had seen and done all over again.

'Very clear,' said the policeman. 'It's important that you actually saw these men moving the sheep and putting them in the truck. It's evidence, that is. Good, solid evidence. We'll need to take a statement from you all.'

'Yes, but not now,' said Mrs Jones firmly. 'These girls and boys are coming back to the farm with me for a hot drink and some food. They've had a tough night.'

'But we have to get our bikes,' said Connor as the officers escorted two of the four men to the police car, their hands in handcuffs. 'We have to go back to the campsite. It's the middle of the night. We can't stay for a meal.'

'Nonsense,' said Mrs Jones. 'After all that running around in the dark I'm not letting you go back without a bite to eat.'

'I'll take you back on the trailer afterwards,' her husband said. 'We'll put the bikes on it. You're not telling me you have the energy to cycle up that hill again?'

'Well, no,' said Connor, who suddenly felt very tired indeed. 'I don't think I do. But the road's blocked by the truck.'

'We'll go through the fields,' Mrs Jones said.

'There's an old track that comes out a bit further along.'

'You mean, we didn't have to go down by the river?' said Abby. 'We didn't have to go through the cows' field?'

'No,' said the farmer. 'But you weren't to know. There's no Public Right of Way up here.'

'We've sent for reinforcements,' said the officer, returning. 'They'll take the other two prisoners into custody and they'll move these vehicles. I hope you lot won't make a habit out of letting tyres down. Not the sort of thing you expect from Scouts.'

'No,' began Connor, 'we—'

'I'm joking,' said the policeman. 'You've done a terrific job tonight, all of you. There's a lot of farmers in this valley who will be very grateful to you.'

'Well, then,' said Mrs Jones to the officer. 'We'll leave you to sort things out here and I'll get these young folk fed. Into the car, all of you.'

CHAPTER 16

Back at the farmhouse, Mrs Jones made the Tigers sit round her enormous kitchen table while she heated milk on a massive black stove. 'This is milk from our own cows,' she said.

'Not the ones down near the river?' asked Abby.

'That's right.' Mrs Jones smiled. 'We don't have many. It was our son's idea. There's a cheese factory down the valley and most of the milk goes there. We just keep a little for ourselves. It makes very good cocoa. Here you are . . .'

She put steaming mugs in front of the Scouts. Priya sipped hers eagerly. It was delicious and incredibly creamy.

The door opened and Mr Jones came in. 'I gave the dogs a little treat,' he said. 'It's not every night that they arrest a bunch of crooks.'

'I don't understand how they rounded them up on their own,' said Toby. 'You weren't even there.'

'To tell you the truth, I sometimes think old Meg could run the farm on her own, she's that clever. She knows what I want her to do before I even tell her.'

Mrs Jones put out the remains of the apple pie they'd had earlier, along with a large fruitcake. Priya discovered to her surprise that she was actually hungry – the fruitcake was delicious. It was obvious that the others agreed. They all munched happily between sips of cocoa.

'And now, Thomas,' said Mrs Jones at last, 'you'd better take these young people back to their beds. Look at them yawning. Make sure you call in and see us tomorrow, won't you?'

'Of course,' said Connor. 'But it's tomorrow already, isn't it?'

They all waited in the yard while Mr Jones fetched the tractor and trailer. The moon had sunk towards the distant mountains and the sky above them was bright with stars.

'The sheep!' said Priya suddenly. 'The one with the poorly leg. Is she all right? Can we see her?'

'She's fine,' said Mrs Jones as the tractor drew up beside them. 'I'll tell her you were asking after her. Now off you go. And thank you, all of you, for what you've done.'

The Tigers sat in the trailer, cushioned on bales of fresh, sweet-smelling hay. Mr Jones took a stony track straight up the hillside, then turned off towards the head of the valley. Suddenly they could see everything spread out below them in the moonlight – the distant shadowy hills, and the river like a silver snake in the valley bottom.

'It's very beautiful,' murmured Priya. 'It's like a dream.'

'Well, it's not a dream,' replied Abby. 'I've never been this tired in a dream.'

The tractor turned downhill and they soon

joined the road again. Mr Jones made them stay in the trailer while he handed their bikes up to them. They drove on past the empty farm and up the steep hill to the campsite.

'There you are, then,' the farmer said when they had parked their bikes. 'This all looks very neat and cosy. You'd better get off to sleep. And thank you again. We're really very, very grateful.' He shook hands with each of them before climbing onto the tractor and driving away.

'Look,' said Priya. 'I think it's starting to get light.'

'We could stay up and see the sunrise,' suggested Jay.

'You're forgetting,' Connor pointed out. 'We have to get up at seven o'clock and cycle forty kilometres in the morning. We have to complete the mission.'

'Well, one thing's for sure,' said Andy, who was already crawling into his tent. 'No one can say we haven't found out about how people live in the valley. I hope my great-grandparents were like Mr and Mrs Jones.'

Priya wriggled into her sleeping bag. When she closed her eyes, she could still see the moonlit valley and the dappled shade under the trees by the river. She felt as if her head were full of moonlight.

'Hey,' whispered Abby. 'What happened to being scared of the darkness?'

'There was no time,' replied Priya sleepily. 'There was no time to be scared. And anyway, it was never dark, not really – it was . . .'

But she never finished her sentence.

Quite suddenly, she was asleep.

And then, even more suddenly, she was wide awake. The sun was hot on the side of the tent and birds were singing outside. She had been dreaming. Or had it really happened? She blinked, and then she realized – they had to cycle home. They should have been up early, and it definitely wasn't early now. She fumbled for her watch and saw to her horror that it was nearly half-past nine.

She shook Abby's shoulder. 'Wake up!' she said. 'We've overslept. Connor!' she called. 'Toby! Everyone! It's nine-thirty!'

They all stumbled out of their tents in a panic, rubbing their eyes in the hot sunshine.

'I don't believe it,' Connor exclaimed. 'None of us set our alarms.'

'I did,' said Toby. 'But my watch was under my sleeping bag and I didn't hear it.'

'Well, it doesn't matter now,' said Jay. 'We can still catch the train. We'll just have to cycle fast, that's all. And there is one good thing. It's down-hill nearly all the way.'

'Jay's right,' agreed Andy. 'We can do it. It really *will* be like the Tour de France.'

'OK,' said Connor. 'But we still have to do everything properly. Andy, you and Jay get the fire going and make the porridge. Abby, you tidy up the wood-chopping area and put the rest of the wood back in the shelter. The rest of us will be taking the tents down and packing up. OK?'

'But we haven't got time for porridge,' said Andy, rubbing his eyes sleepily.

'Yes, we have,' replied Connor. 'That's what we brought for breakfast and we'll need good food inside us if we're going to cycle all that way.'

Abby and Priya worked quickly to stuff their sleeping bags away and roll up their mats. Priya put her bag outside, and Abby went off to sort out the wood, leaving Priya to take down the tent. She carefully collected the pegs and put them in the bag, then remembered to push the poles out of the sleeves. By the time Abby returned, all the tents were packed away and porridge was bubbling in Toby's large billycan over a crackling fire.

'That's one good thing about oversleeping,' said Connor with a grin as Toby slopped the porridge into bowls. 'At least the sun had time to dry out the tents.'

They ate the porridge quickly, then poured water on the embers of the fire and covered it with earth. They strapped everything to the bikes, put on their helmets, and took a final look around the campsite.

'Exactly the way we found it,' said Connor. 'That's perfect. It's ten thirty now and the train's at one thirty. Forty kilometres in three hours. We'll just have time.'

'We've got to stop at the farm, don't forget,' Priya reminded him. 'We can't leave without saying goodbye.'

'Then we'd better get moving. Why don't you go first, Priya? It's time you had a turn in front.'

Priya jumped on her bike and pedalled quickly to the entrance. She checked both ways and set off down the road. It was a great feeling, swooping down the hill with no one else in front of her. Just in time, she remembered to brake for the steepest part of the descent, then she was off again, pedalling as hard as she could, over the bridge and up the gentle slope away from the river, past the place where they had split up the night before.

There were the woods away to her left, and there was the field of cows. They were lying down in the sun, and Priya just had time to wonder if they always stayed awake at night before she saw the farm entrance ahead of her. She stood on the pedals and raced up the track into the yard. The dogs came running towards her, tongues flopping out, almost as if they were smiling.

'They're not barking,' said Jay. 'You didn't half go fast! I could hardly keep up.'

Priya nodded, too out of breath to talk, as the others arrived.

Mrs Jones appeared in the doorway of the farmhouse. 'The dogs know you now,' she said, smiling broadly.

Priya felt a cold nose touch her hand; she looked down and saw Meg looking up at her.

'I thought you'd be here long before this,' Mrs Jones said. 'Didn't you tell me you had a train to catch?'

'We do,' replied Connor. 'We all overslept. I'm

really sorry, Mrs Jones, but we can't stop. The train is at one-thirty.'

'Goodness me,' she exclaimed. 'Well, look, I've got a little something for you for the journey. It won't take me a second. Thomas!' she shouted. 'Where have you got to? The children are here!' And she disappeared into the house.

Priya ran over to the stable and looked over the half-door to see the injured sheep staring up at her and letting out a deep Baaaa.

'Not much wrong with her,' Mr Jones said, coming up behind her with the other Tigers. 'You lot should get a special Sheep Savers badge, if you ask me. Or maybe a Farm Savers badge. They should invent one specially for you. I'm going to write to your Scout Leader and tell him so.'

'You don't have to do that,' Connor said. 'After all, what else could we have done?'

'You could have got back in your tents and gone to sleep, that's what,' said the farmer. 'I'm not letting you leave this farmyard until I know how to get in touch with you again. And if you ever want to come and camp in that meadow, you'll be very welcome.'

'Here,' said Mrs Jones. 'I've packed up some fruitcake. And these are some of our own cheeses. One for each of you.'

They stowed her gifts carefully in their panniers and Connor wrote Rick's details and his own in Mr Jones's address book.

'Don't forget,' the farmer said. 'The police will be wanting to talk to you.'

'We're used to that,' said Jay. 'I don't know why, but whenever we do anything together we seem to end up talking to the police!'

Mr and Mrs Jones were both laughing as Priya set off down the track again. She glanced over her shoulder and saw that all five dogs were running beside them. The Tigers turned onto the road and the dogs stood watching as they cycled away down the valley.

'OK,' said Connor. 'We've got two hours. Let's not spoil everything by missing the train!'

* * *

Connor felt as if he was flying down the valley. Not only was it downhill all the way, but a gusty breeze had sprung up behind them and almost seemed to be pushing them along.

'We're doing thirty-five kph,' Jay called over his shoulder as they raced past the spot where Connor had been knocked off his bike.

'I'm in top gear!' cried Abby from behind him. 'I wish I had a higher one.'

They passed the farm where they'd seen the herd of cows, and crossed the bridge. There was a gentle climb that felt like no climb at all with the wind behind them, and then a long cruise downhill until suddenly Priya cried out: 'I can see the main road!' and Connor saw the glint of sunlight on the cars and trucks passing to and fro. And there, beyond the road, was the little town. He breathed a sigh of relief. They were going to make the train with time to spare.

'Hey, Connor!' yelled Abby from behind him. 'You dropped something!'

'Wait, everyone,' Connor called as she caught up with him. 'What was it?'

'Don't know,' she said. 'I think it fell out of your pocket.'

Connor gulped. His pocket was unzipped and his wallet had dropped out. He could see it lying on the road a hundred metres back. 'Thanks, Abby,' he said. 'It's got our tickets in and everything. That could have been a disaster.'

He turned his bike to cycle back up the road and instantly found himself battling a fierce wind in completely the wrong gear. He slipped down into his lowest gear and still had to work hard. 'You know what?' he said to the others as he rejoined them. 'We've been really lucky. If that wind had been blowing the other way we would never have made it.'

'We still haven't,' said Toby. 'I won't feel happy until we're sitting on that train.'

Three hours later, Tiger Patrol arrived back at Matfield station.

'We've done it,' Connor said to the others as they unloaded their bikes. 'We've completed the Expedition Challenge.'

'And I've got some great footage of the land of my forefathers,' announced Andy grandly.

'What do you mean?' asked Abby. 'Who are your forefathers then, the sheep – or the cows?'

'Ha, ha,' said Andy. 'So everything's back to normal, now we're back in the real world.'

'There's Rick and Julie,' said Jay suddenly. 'And my mum and dad.'

'It looks like *all* our parents have come to welcome us back,' added Toby, spotting his mum in the crowd.

Connor saw his dad behind them all. He must have driven fast, he thought, because he'd been sure he'd caught a glimpse of him outside the station in Wales. Dr Sutcliff gave Connor a big thumbs-up and a wave.

Mr and Mrs Gupta ran over to Priya and Mr Gupta held her bike while she hugged her mum.

'How was it?' Mrs Gupta asked. 'You didn't have to send for help, then?'

'Priya was fantastic,' Connor said. 'I reckon she's probably the toughest Tiger of us all. And she tells great campfire stories too.'

'Ah,' said Mr Gupta proudly. 'She gets that from me.'

Rick raised a hand for silence. 'Welcome back, Tiger Patrol,' he said. 'I'm looking forward to hearing your report on your mission. It sounds as if you've done enough to get your Expedition Challenge Award.'

There was a cheer from the assembled parents, and the members of Tiger Patrol exchanged high-fives.

'It's great to see you all back safe and sound,' continued Rick. 'And we're all very pleased that, just for once, you've managed to have a nice, straightforward expedition without too much excitement.'

A phone began to ring in his pocket. 'Yes?' he said, answering the call. 'This is the Sixth

Matfield Scout Leader . . . You're calling from Wales . . . ? Tiger Patrol did what . . . ?'

The Tigers and their parents waited. Occasionally Rick asked a question, but mostly he just listened, with an expression of growing astonishment on his face. Finally he ended the call, shaking his head. 'I take it all back,' he told the Tigers. 'That was a Mr Jones. I'm not sure I understood everything he said, but it sounds as if there's an awful lot you haven't told us yet, Connor.'

'Well,' said Connor, looking at the others and smiling, 'it was like this . . .'

PARAGLIDING Notes from Connor

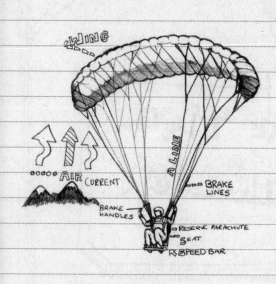

Paragliders are lightweight aircraft which are usually launched on foot.

The pilot sits in a harness below the wing.

Paragliders don't have engines but they can sometimes fly for hours and travel hundreds of kilometres.

Paragliders can climb several thousand metres by using thermals. Thermals are columns of rising air. They are often caused when the sun warms the land.

You can find out if you'd enjoy paragliding by taking a tandem flight where you sit in a harness in front of the pilot.

LOOKING AFTER YOUR BIKE (1) Notes from Priya

Lubricating your bike

Once a month you should check, clean and
lubricate the moving parts of your bike with oil
or a lubricant spray. I've labelled the parts you
should lubricate:

1. Front and rear derailleur assemblies
2. Chain
3. Gear and brake cables and adjusters
4. Gear and brake levers/changers
5. The moving parts of brakes (but make sure you
   don't get oil on the brake blocks or wheel rims!)
6. Pedals

Top tips for when you have a puncture

1. Always carry a spare inner tube. You can get moving again quickly and fix the puncture when you get home. It's no fun patching an inner tube in the cold or the wet!

2. Be very careful when taking the tyre off and replacing it that you don't damage it with the tyre levers.

3. Always check the inside of the tyre before putting the new tube in. Whatever caused the puncture might still be stuck in the tyre. But be careful — whatever it is will be sharp!

4. If you do have to patch a tube follow the instructions on the puncture repair kit — and don't forget to take one with you!

CHOOSING A GOOD PLACE TO PUT UP YOUR TENT.

Notes from Abby

1. You need somewhere that's dry and level.
2. Watch out for low-lying spots and hollows in the ground. If it rains they might fill up with water.
3. Don't camp under trees if you can help it. They keep the rain off at first, but it keeps on dripping from the trees long after it's stopped raining. And the sun can't dry out your tent.
4. Clifftops and very exposed places aren't good either. If the wind gets up you might be blown away!
5. Check that the ground is soft enough to get your tent pegs in. Remove anything sharp or lumpy that might damage the groundsheet.

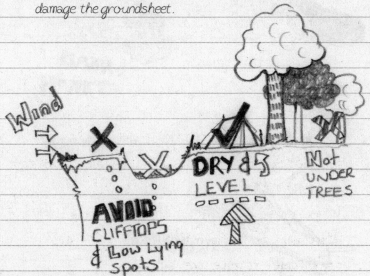

USEFUL THINGS FOR CAMPING Notes from Andy

1. Headtorch
2. Penknife
3. Lightweight fork and spoon (or a Spork!)
4. Lightweight mug and bowl
5. Collapsible kitchen sink (if you're Toby!)
6. Sleeping mat
7. Sleeping bag
8. Inflatable pillow (if you're Toby!)
9. Food
10. Water

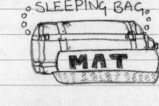

EXPEDITION FOOD Notes from Toby

We planned our expedition food carefully.

DAY 1

On the train: Choc bar, fruit, water

Lunch: Sandwiches, cake, fruit, water

Afternoon snack: Banana (or whatever other fruit each of us brought) survival cake (Connor's grandpa's recipe). Actually, we ate even more because of Mr and Mrs Jones!

Supper: Baked potato, cheese, baked beans with sausages (we took the cans home with us), fruit, hot chocolate

DAY 2

Breakfast: Porridge with sugar, tea or coffee

Lunch: We were going to buy burgers but we ran out of time. Luckily we had Mrs Jones's fruit cake to eat.

WATER

FRUIT

SURVIVAL CAKE

TRAIL MIX

SANDWICH

Regular safety checks

Every time you ride you should check:

1. Are the tyres correctly inflated? Can you see any signs of damage on the tyres?
2. Are the brakes working properly? Check for wear on brake blocks.
3. Is the chain running smoothly through the gears, and are the gears working properly?
4. Are the gear and brake cables in good condition?
5. Are the handlebars and saddle fixed securely?
6. Are there any rattles or noises that shouldn't be there?
7. You should also check your helmet for any signs of damage.

CYCLIST
ACTIVITY BADGE

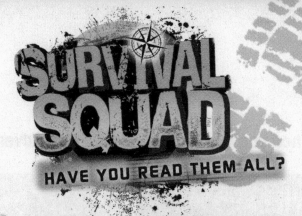

SURVIVAL SQUAD

HAVE YOU READ THEM ALL?

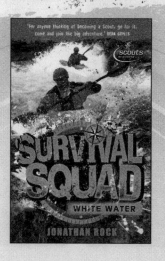

IT'S TIGER PATROL'S TOUGHEST CHALLENGE YET!

FROM SNOW RESCUES TO MIDNIGHT BIKE RIDES AND MYSTERY, SURVIVAL SQUAD ARE ALWAYS UP FOR A CHALLENGE.

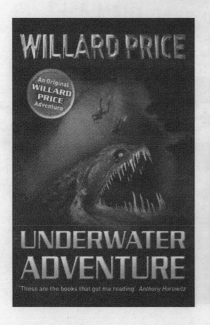 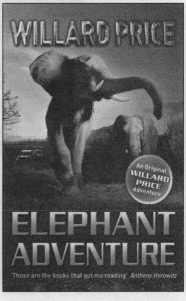